For Brian and our girls. I love you all!
Thank you for dreaming with me.
—A.J.

To my mom and dad, who always believed in me, who pushed me to follow this path, and who allowed me to realize my dreams.
—K.L.

Adventures in the Friendly Forest

Adventures in the Friendly Forest

A 30-DAY STORYBOOK DEVOTIONAL
to Help Kids Grow in Faith and Character

WRITTEN BY
Amanda Jass

ILLUSTRATED BY
Katya Longhi

DAY		
1	Change Blows Through the Friendly Forest	8
2	Hensley Trades Fear for Faith	14
3	Hoo Learns to Open Up	18
4	Slow Down, Blaze!	23
5	Cubby Leaves Space for Grace	27
6	Flora Finds Confidence	32
7	Hensley Turns Worries into Prayers	36
8	Cubby Gives Up His Cozy Comforts	41
9	Hey, Hoo, You're Made to Be You!	45
10	Flora and the Wheelbarrow Disaster	50
11	Be Brave, Hensley!	54
12	Hoo Learns About Gratitude	58
13	Choosing Friendship over Fighting	62
14	Hensley (Finally) Asks for Help	66
15	Left Out or Invited In	70
16	Blaze Learns About Self-Control	75
17	The Forest Friends Find Joy	79
18	The Forest Friends Serve Others	84
19	Ask Your Questions, Flora	88
20	Blaze Needs to Practice Patience	93
21	Cubby Tells the Truth	97
22	Hoo's Forgiveness Dilemma	101
23	What Will Flora Follow?	106
24	Hensley Does the Next Right Thing	110
25	You Can Be Kind, Cubby	115
26	Wise Up, Blaze!	119
27	Flora's Lost Scarf	124
28	Hensley, You're Not Forgotten	128
29	The Forest Friends Find Hope	132
30	The Friendly Forest Celebrates!	136

Hi, there!

I'm so glad you picked up this storybook about the Friendly Forest! Something really special about this book is it's not just stories—each day (or chapter) is actually a devotional to help you learn and grow in your faith.

Every day, you can read one chapter, which includes a forest friends' adventure, a key Bible verse, some reflection questions, and a short prayer. But if you ever want to read through just the stories, you can do that, too, because together they make up one big story about the Friendly Forest!

Like the forest friends you'll meet in these pages, you might be dealing with big changes around you. Or maybe you're just looking for some faith-filled fun. Either way, I hope you enjoy adventuring alongside Blaze, Hensley, Hoo, Cubby, and Flora.

And remember, even though these stories are fiction or "make-believe," they can help you learn lots of important things about who God created you to be. And unlike these stories, God *isn't* make-believe. He's real, He's powerful, and He loves you so much!

Amanda

DAY 1

Change Blows Through the Friendly Forest

The grass dries up. The flowers fall to the ground. But what our God says will stand forever.

ISAIAH 40:8, NIRV

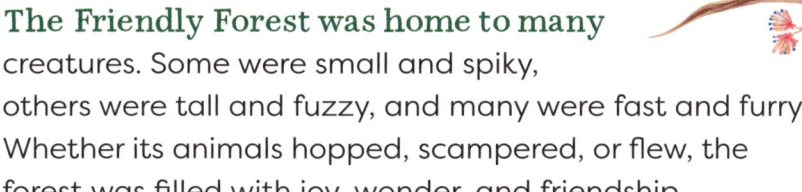

The Friendly Forest was home to many creatures. Some were small and spiky, others were tall and fuzzy, and many were fast and furry. Whether its animals hopped, scampered, or flew, the forest was filled with joy, wonder, and friendship.

Cubby the Bear loved finding the best honey for his grammy's bakery.

Hensley the Hedgehog enjoyed exploring along the Babbling Brook.

Blaze the Bunny hopped around the forest with speed, making special deliveries.

Flora the Fox happily cheered as her friends played games at Frontier's Field.

And Hoo the Owl flew in and out of the trees on calm, starry nights.

But one night, a huge storm blew through the forest. The wind was too strong for Hoo to fly through the skies. Branches rattled and snapped, making Hensley shake in her nest. The pounding rain came down faster than Blaze could think. Crashing thunder startled Flora from her sleep, and lightning lit up the doorway of Cubby's den.

The next morning, the creatures of the Friendly Forest woke up to find that their happy little home looked completely different. All the trails were washed out. The North Bridge had been swept away. And the forest was now filled with questions, confusion, and lots of fear.

But even though their world had changed, the forest friends were about to discover an important truth. No matter what was happening around them or what emotions the storm had brought to the surface, each of them could *choose* how to respond. And those choices could eventually change everything.

Talk About It

- What is the big change that happened in the Friendly Forest?
- Read Isaiah 40:8 again. What truth does this verse share about God?
- Do you like it when things around you change? Why or why not?

Think About It

While the things in this world will change, we can trust that God never changes! He will always love you, and He will always be with you.

Pray About It

Dear God,

Thank You for loving me and being with me every day. Please help me remember that even when things change, You and Your Word stay the same.

Amen.

DAY
2

Hensley Trades Fear for Faith

Trust in the Lord with all your heart;
do not depend on your own understanding.

PROVERBS 3:5

Hensley was curled up tight in her nest, like she did when something was really, *really* wrong. It took a long time for her to say anything to Mama Hedgehog, who sat by Hensley's side.

"That storm was so loud last night," Hensley finally squeaked out.

"It sure was." Mama Hedgehog kissed her cheek. "Thankfully we stayed safe and sound."

"But I'm scared that the forest won't be okay." Papa Hedgehog had left early that morning to help the families in the Western Woodland. He said they all had to work hard to fix the forest before winter came. Otherwise, they'd have to leave and find a new home. "The storm changed everything! I don't like it!" Hensley cried.

"Change is hard," said Mama Hedgehog. "But I'm here for you, and so are your friends. And most importantly, the Maker is watching over you."

Hensley loosened from her ball a bit. "Really?"

"Really!" said Mama. "No matter what changes here on earth, the Maker never changes. He is always loving,

He is always there, and He is always good."

"Will the Maker help me not be afraid ever again?" asked Hensley.

"You'll probably still feel afraid at times," Mama explained. "But when you do, you can ask the Maker to help you trade your fear for faith. And then you can keep choosing faith over and over again."

Hensley thought about Mama's words. Then she took a deep breath and fully unfurled from her ball. "Okay, Mama. I'm still a little afraid, but I'll try to have faith."

Talk About It

- Why was Hensley scared in today's story?
- What does it mean to have faith and to trust our Maker (God)?
- What will you choose to trust God with today?

Think About It

Hopefully you have people you can trust here on earth when things around you are changing. But no matter what, remember that you can always trust God!

Pray About It

Dear God,

Please help me have faith in You, even when I don't like what's changing around me. When I feel alone or afraid, help me remember that You are still here with me.

Amen.

DAY 3

Hoo Learns to Open Up

Share each other's burdens, and in this way obey the law of Christ.
GALATIANS 6:2

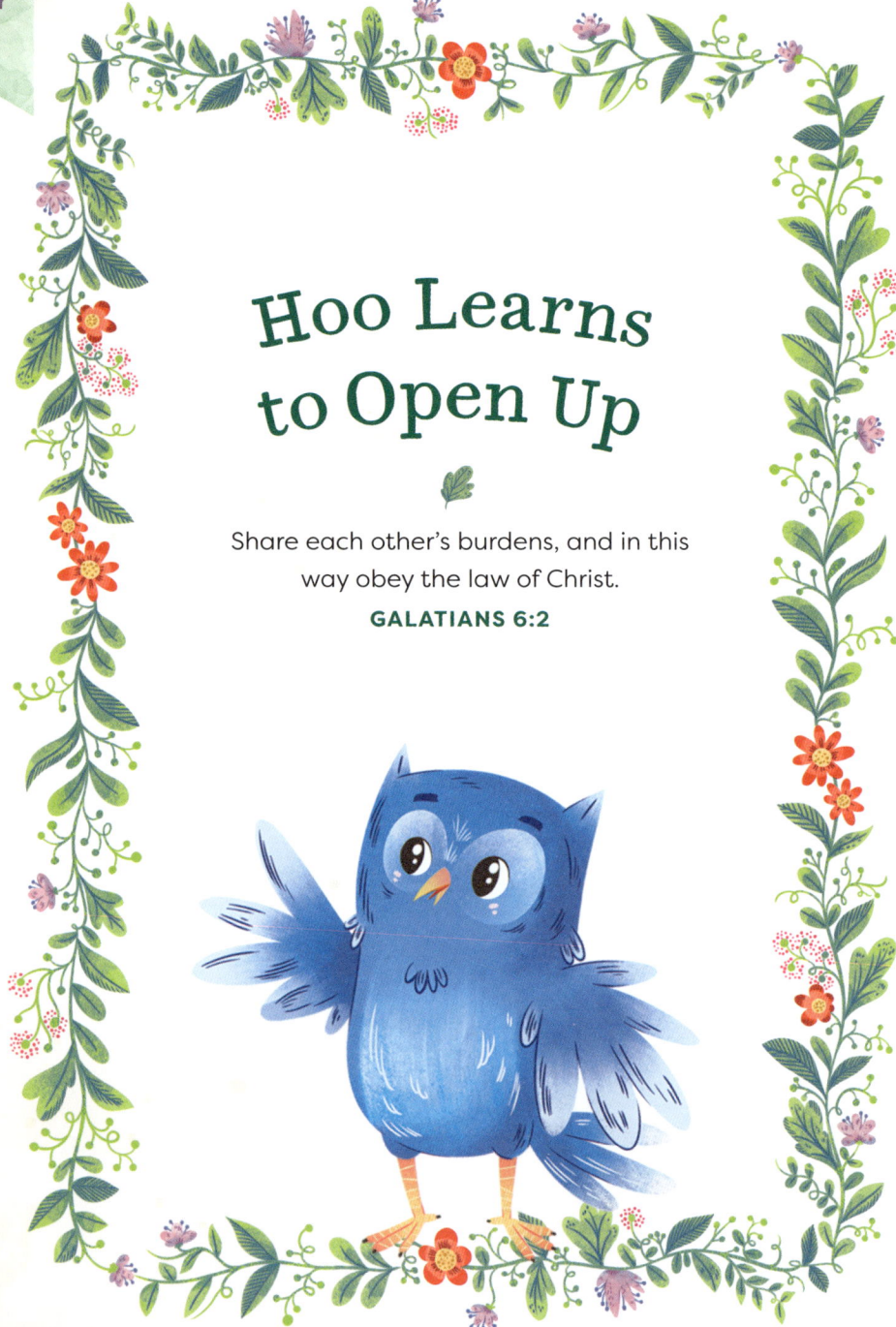

Hoo hooted sadly as he perched on a broken tree branch.

"What's wrong, Hoo?" asked Hensley.

"Oh, it's nothing to bother you about," answered Hoo as he flew to a higher branch. But a few minutes later, he let out a loud wail and a few sad, sniffly hoots.

"Come down here, Hoo," called Hensley. "It sounds like you could use a friend."

Hoo continued to "hoo-hoo" sadly as he flew down. Yet no matter how many ways Hensley asked him what was wrong, Hoo would only sniffle in response.

Finally Hensley said, "It's okay to be sad. Maybe if you talk about it, you'll feel better. That's what happened to me when I told Mama about being afraid."

"I don't want to moo-hoo-ooove," Hoo eventually sobbed.

He told Hensley about his old tree, which had been knocked down in the storm. And even though his parents had already found a new one, it was on the other side of the Babbling Brook! "It's too far away from everything I'm used to," Hoo finished.

"Change can feel scary sometimes," said Hensley. "Hmm, maybe we can think of something cool about your new tree."

Hoo thought for a moment, then piped up, "I can swoop right over the brook and get to Grammy's Bakery in seventeen-point-two seconds!"

"Wait. Is your tree the big pine near Critter Crossing?" asked Hensley.

"Yes," Hoo replied.

"Hooray!" shouted Hensley. "We'll be next-door neighbors!"

Hoo's eyes grew even wider than usual, and he fluffed his feathers. He was still a bit sad he had to move, but this was the best news he'd heard all week!

Talk About It

- Why was Hoo sad in today's story?
- How did Hoo feel after he talked to Hensley about moving?
- Who could you open up to about something that's been bothering you?

Think About It

We can always talk to God about the changes going on within or around us. We don't need to keep everything inside. And remember, God places people in our lives we can open up to as well!

Pray About It

Dear God,

Thank You for giving me family and friends to talk with. Help me open up to You and to others who love me.

Amen.

DAY 4

Slow Down, Blaze!

Slow down. Take a deep breath.
What's the hurry?
Why wear yourself out? Just what
are you after anyway?

JEREMIAH 2:25, MSG

Blaze raced around the Friendly Forest. Everywhere he looked, there was something to do and someone to help.

Like Mr. Owl! Hoo's dad was having a hard time getting a rocking chair into their new tree. "Hiya, Mr. Owl! I can get something super-de-duper to help you!" Blaze said. And then he zoomed off before Mr. Owl could respond.

But then Blaze smacked into Grammy Bear. She was searching in the shadows for more blueberries to add to her pie.

"Sorry about bumping you, Grammy," Blaze said. "But I have a spectacular-ific device to light up your baking nights!" Blaze was out of sight before Grammy could say "Thank you."

The bunny booked it from here to there at lightning speed. He zoomed back toward Grammy, dropping off a small saw. Then he zoomed over to Mr. Owl, tossing him a lantern. He was about to race off to the next to-do, but Mr. Owl flew right in his path.

"I appreciate the thought, Blaze, but I don't know what I'd use a lantern for. Owls see best in the dark!"

Oops! The lantern was for Grammy. Just then Grammy walked over with the saw and a confused look. Oops again!

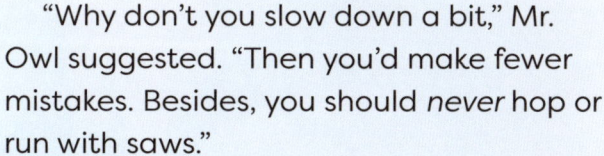

"Why don't you slow down a bit," Mr. Owl suggested. "Then you'd make fewer mistakes. Besides, you should *never* hop or run with saws."

Grammy agreed. "I've become quite good at taking things slow, Blaze. Come by the bakery sometime and I'll show you."

"Deal!" Blaze started to speed off but tripped over his own tangled-up feet. "Umm, does right now work, Grammy?"

Talk About It

- Why do you think Blaze was in such a rush?
- Do you ever have a hard time slowing down when you're going about your day?
- Why might God want us to slow down at times?

Think About It

It can be good to work hard and move quickly, but God knows we need to sometimes move more slowly. God created us to work, to play, *and* to rest!

Pray About It

Dear God,

Please help me remember that it's sometimes good to slow down and take breaks. Thank You for giving us times for work and times for rest.

Amen.

DAY 5

Cubby Leaves Space for Grace

He said to me, "My grace is sufficient for you, for my power is made perfect in weakness."

2 CORINTHIANS 12:9, NIV

Cubby loved helping at his grammy's bakery. Today when he walked in, he noticed Blaze pulling a berry crisp out of the oven.

Berry juice oozed out the sides, and the topping was burnt. *That's not a perfect crisp,* Cubby thought. *Grammy can't sell that one.* Cubby decided he'd show Blaze how it was done by making a pecan pie with bear-y good honey drizzle.

After several long minutes, Blaze said, "Cubby, you've been rolling out that crust for *forever.*"

"It's got to be . . . perfect!" Cubby replied, finally pleased with his work. He oh-so-carefully poured the pecan filling before starting the honey drizzle.

"Oh fiddlesticks!" Cubby muttered.

"What's wrong?" Grammy asked.

"This drizzle is too runny!" Cubby added more honey. "Grr—now it's too sticky!"

"It doesn't need to be perfect," said Grammy. "Perfection leaves no space for grace."

But Cubby wasn't going to stop until it was just right. He stirred faster . . . and *faster* . . . and FASTER!

"Slow down!" shouted Blaze.

Shocked to hear those words from Blaze, Cubby stopped stirring, but the drizzle didn't stop swirling. It flew up until . . . *Plop!* The sticky goo splattered Grammy squarely in the face.

"I ruined everything!" Cubby cried as he and Blaze hurried to help Grammy.

"You did make a mess." Grammy chuckled while wiping a glob of goo from her forehead. "But you can try again. And as you give yourself grace, remember the amazing grace the Maker offers!"

Cubby nodded, starting the drizzle again.

Later that afternoon, the space-for-grace pie came out of the oven looking *and* tasting pretty perfect after all.

Talk About It

- What was Cubby upset about in the story?
- Do you ever get upset when you don't do everything perfectly?
- Read 2 Corinthians 12:9 again. How is God's power made perfect?

Think About It

Remember, God knows we're not perfect, but He loves us anyway. Like today's verse says, God's power is made perfect in our weaknesses—which includes our imperfections!

Pray About It

Dear God,

Please help me remember that I don't need to be perfect. Thank You for giving us grace even when we mess things up.

Amen.

DAY 6

Flora Finds Confidence

We are God's creation. He created us to belong to Christ Jesus. Now we can do good works. Long ago God prepared these works for us to do.

EPHESIANS 2:10, NIRV

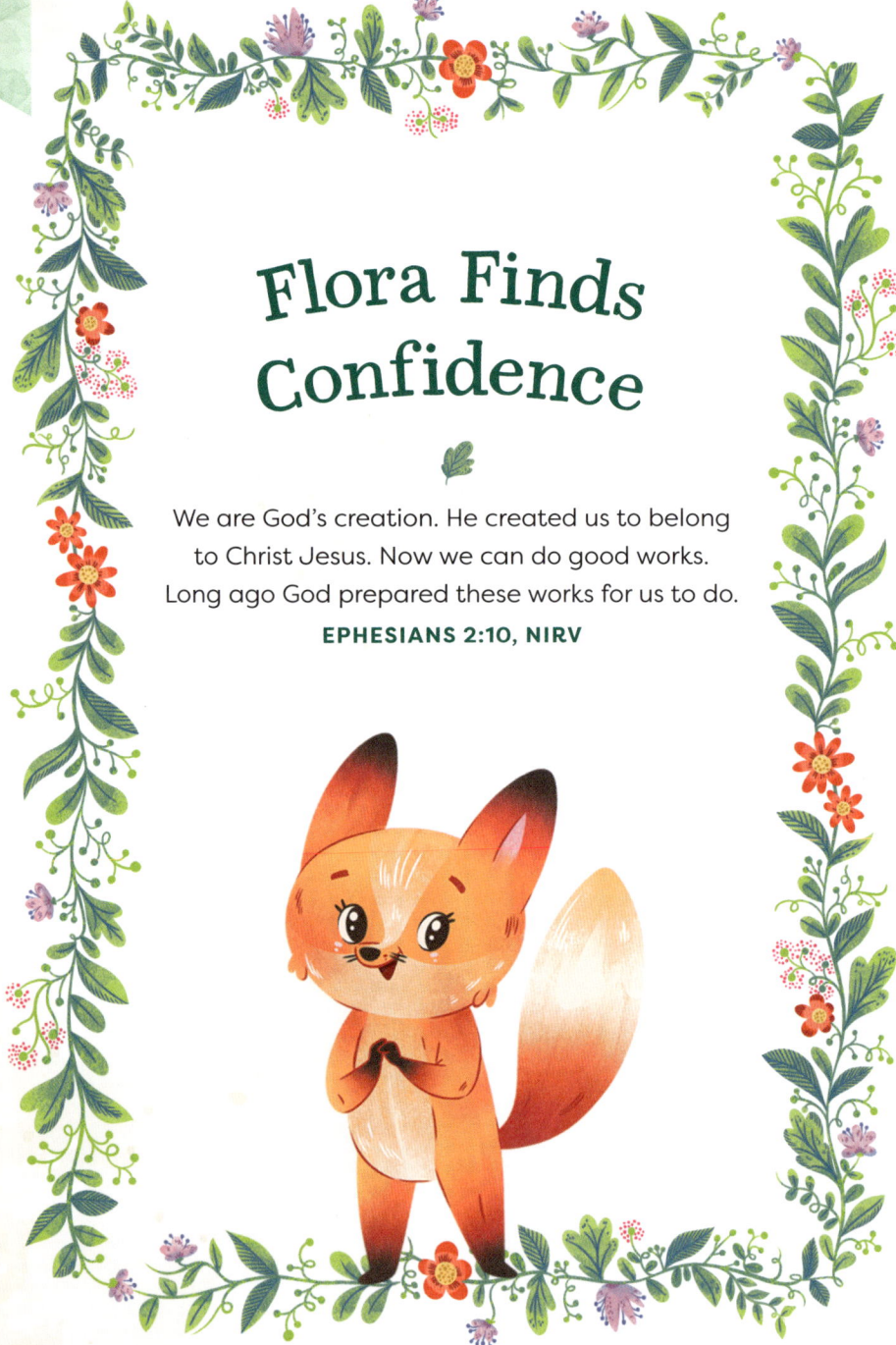

Wherever Flora looked, she saw animals helping with the big storm cleanup in different ways.

She watched Cubby move a fallen tree that was blocking Critter Crossing. "Way to go, Cubby!" Flora cheered. *I wish I were as strong and helpful as Cubby,* she thought.

She watched Hoo map out the plan for the new community garden. "Hoo, you are so wise," Flora told him. But she thought, *I never have any good ideas the way Hoo does.*

She almost crashed into Blaze as he zoomed around making deliveries. "You're the speediest delivery rabbit I've ever seen!" she shouted after him. Foxes were fast, but Flora knew she'd never be as speedy as Blaze.

Everyone has something special they can do, she thought. *Well, everyone except me.*

"What's wrong, Flora?"

Flora opened her puffy, tear-stained eyes to see her friends standing around her. "All of you have such special talents to offer during these forest cleanup days," Flora answered. "And I . . . Well, I have nothing special to help anyone."

Cubby took another step toward his friend. "Flora, instead of comparing yourself to everyone else, how about you start being confident in how the Maker made you?"

"You're the greatest encourager we know," said Hoo. "We couldn't do all this hard work without you-hoo cheering us on."

"And that's why we made you this!" Blaze held up a shiny gold medal.

Flora smiled as she read the inscription: #1 ENCOURAGER. "I guess I do have something to offer after all!"

Talk About It

- Why was Flora feeling discouraged in today's story?
- Do you ever compare yourself to others? How do you feel after you compare?
- Why does God want us to be confident in the way He made us?

Think About It

Remember, you are God's creation. He doesn't want you to get stuck in constantly comparing yourself to others. God made you with your own special skills and talents!

Pray About It

Dear God,

Please help me stop comparing myself to other people. Help me be confident in how you made me, and help me use my talents to serve!

Amen.

DAY 7

Hensley Turns Worries into Prayers

Don't worry about anything; instead, pray about everything. Tell God what you need, and thank him for all he has done.

PHILIPPIANS 4:6

When Mama Hedgehog came to tuck Hensley in, Hensley was talking to her favorite stuffie. "I'm not as scared as I was right after the storm," she said. "But I'm worried about my dad. He's still out helping in the Western Woodland. And what if we all have to leave the Friendly Forest?"

"Hi, sweetie." Mama Hedgehog sat down beside Hensley. "When I'm feeling worried, I like to turn my worries into prayers by talking with the Maker."

"You can do that?" asked Hensley.

"Of course! You can talk to the Maker anytime, anywhere, and about anything," Mama said. "You can talk to your stuffies, but they can't actually hear you because they are make-believe friends. But the Maker *can* hear you, and He loves it when we talk to Him!"

Mama Hedgehog turned out the light as Hensley curled up in her nest. Hensley had never tried talking to the Maker when she was all by herself. What if she said

something silly? Was it too late in the night? Would He even hear her when she was tucked in so tightly?

But then she remembered what her mama just said. She could talk to the Maker anytime about anything—even her worries and questions!

"Dear Maker," she began. "Mama said I can talk to You about anything, and well . . . I'm feeling really worried right now. Please keep my dad safe in the Western Woodland. And please help me trust You. Amen."

Talk About It

- What did Mama Hedgehog say Hensley could do when she was worried?
- God, our Maker, wants us to talk to Him! When and where can we talk to God?
- What are some things that you might want to talk to God about?

Think About It

Remember, you can talk to God anytime, anywhere, and about anything—including your worries. God is always there, and He'll always listen!

Pray About It

Dear God,

Thank You for always listening when I talk to You. Please help me bring my worries to You by praying all throughout my day and even into the night. I love You.

Amen.

DAY 8

Cubby Gives Up His Cozy Comforts

There is no greater love than to lay down one's life for one's friends.

JOHN 15:13

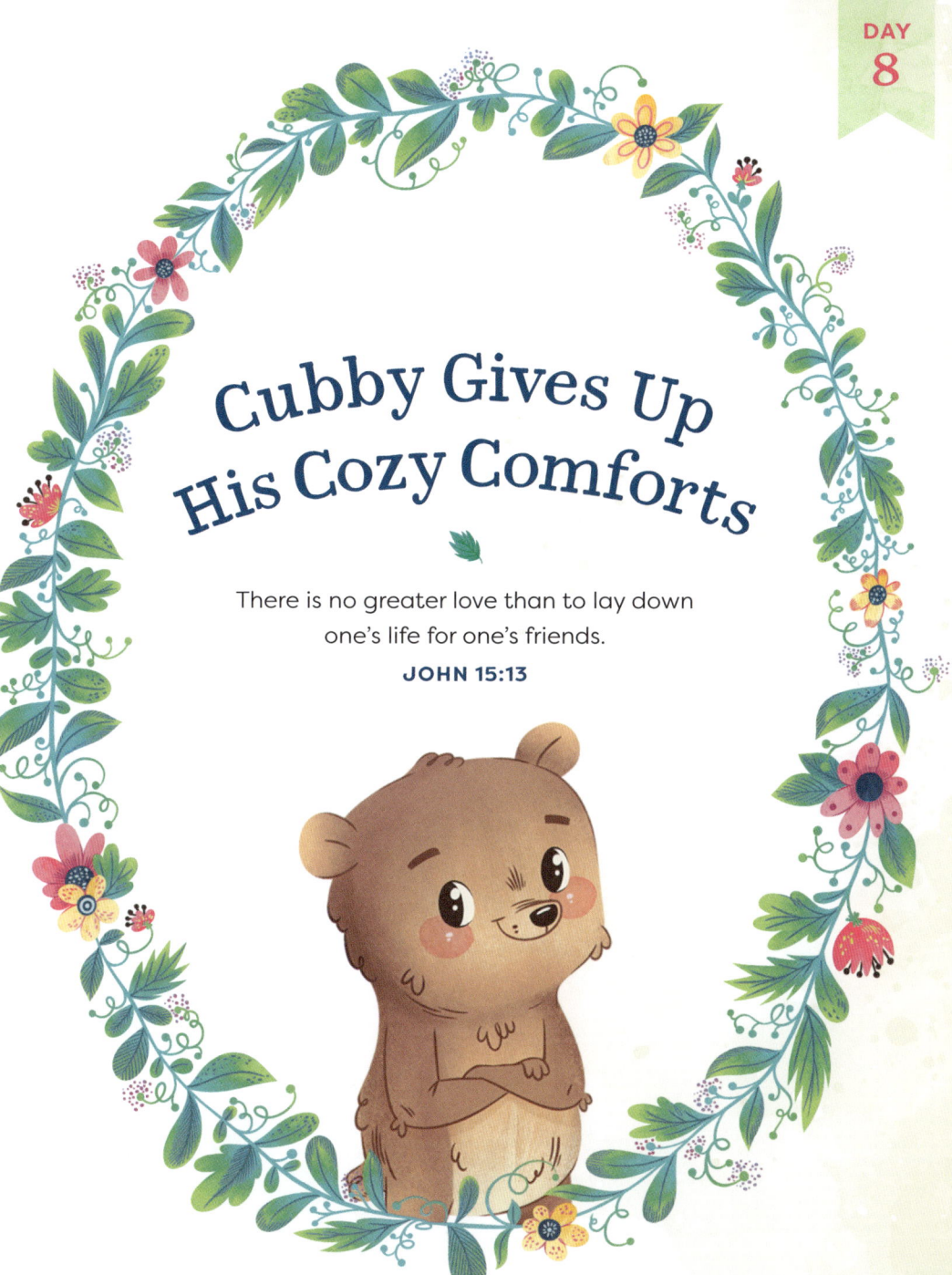

It had been almost a month since the big storm blew through the Friendly Forest, and Cubby had just finished another volunteer shift with the Cleanup Crew.

He was ready to plop into his perfectly made bed in the back of his dark den for a nice long nap. But just as he was about to snuggle in, he heard a sound.

He peeked out his den door, and there was Blaze leaning against a rock, wheezing loudly. Blaze looked more exhausted than Cubby had ever seen him.

"Blaze, are you okay out there?" Cubby asked.

"Oh . . . yes . . . I sure . . . am," Blaze squeaked out between heavy breaths. "Just . . . a few . . . more deliveries."

"If you're sure," answered Cubby, turning back toward his cozy bed. But then he glanced back at Blaze. *That little bunny looks like he might fall right over,* Cubby thought.

"Blaze, why don't I make those last few deliveries and you rest here until I'm back?"

"But you just got home from helping the Cleanup Crew most of the day!" Blaze protested. "And with the North Bridge gone, you'll need to go all the way down to the *South* Bridge to get across the Babbling Brook."

"True, but it looks like you need the shut-eye more than I do," Cubby said. "Plus, the Maker wants us to care for others more than our own little comforts. So stay and rest up, buddy!"

Blaze thanked Cubby before curling up on the den floor and then immediately started snoring away.

Cubby headed out the den door with Blaze's last few deliveries. *It sure feels good to help a friend,* he thought.

Talk About It

- What's the difference between being selfish and selfless?
- How did Cubby choose to be selfless and give up his own comforts?
- What's something you could give up to help someone else this week?

Think About It

We can all get caught up in wanting to do what feels easy or comfortable, but sometimes God wants us to get out of our comfort zones! With God's help, we can go out into the world and show others the same kind of love Jesus shows us.

Pray About It

Dear God,

Thank You for sending Jesus to earth for me. Please help me care for the needs of others over my own cozy comforts. Help me love like Jesus.

Amen.

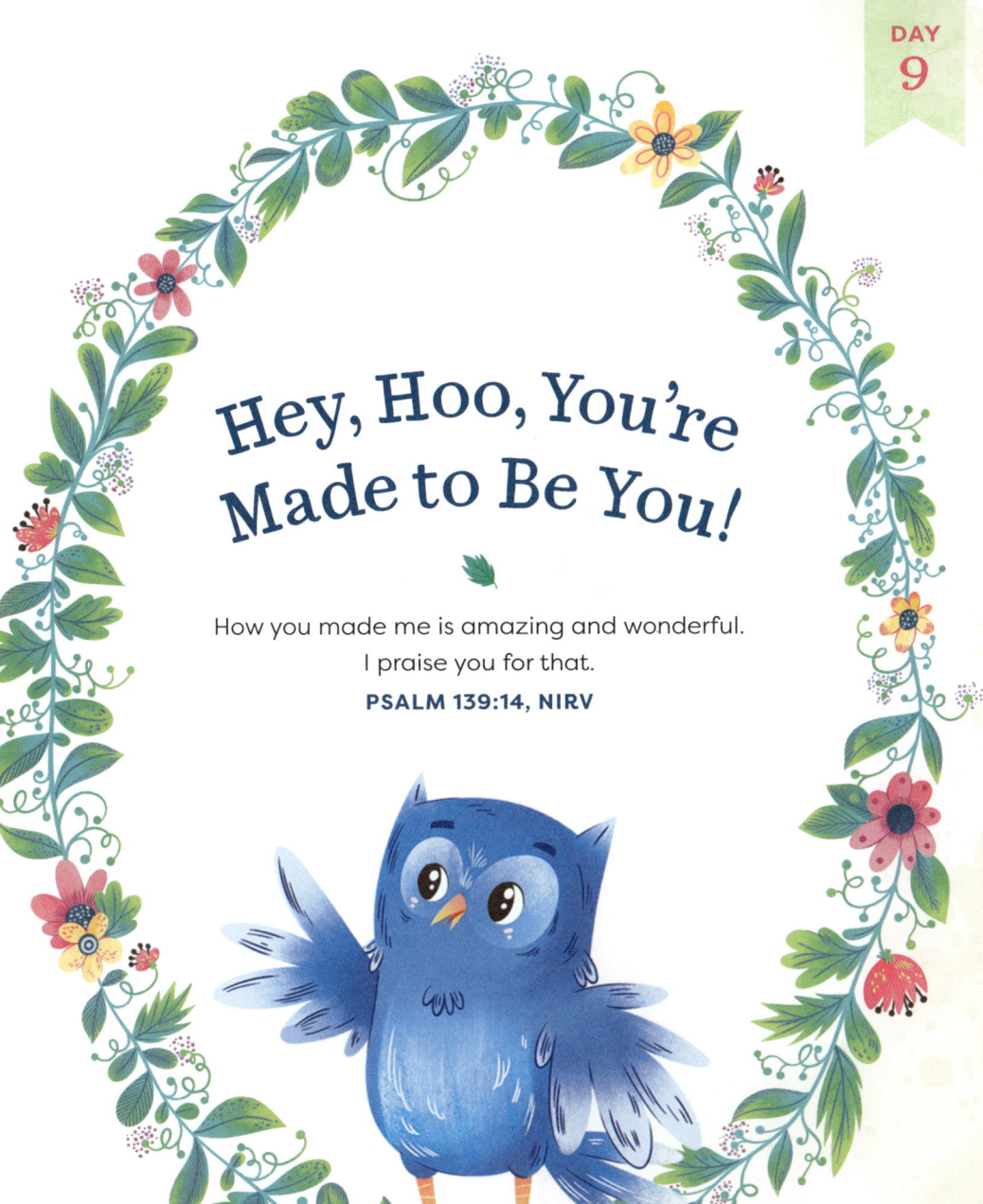

DAY 9

Hey, Hoo, You're Made to Be You!

How you made me is amazing and wonderful.
I praise you for that.
PSALM 139:14, NIRV

One evening while the forest friends were playing tag, Hoo noticed that his friends either scurried, hopped, or walked along the forest floor. He was the only one who flew in the air to get from place to place. And not only that, but he was the only one who was the color blue!

Suddenly Hoo didn't like being a flying blue owl. He gathered a mixture of brown leaves, mud, and powdered sugar from Grammy's Bakery. Then he got to work! Hoo gazed at his reflection, pleased that not a speck of blue could be seen.

Hoo waddled through the forest, spotting Blaze near Thickets and Things with a delivery. Hoo tried to hop (which looked more like a hobble) toward the bunny.

"Aah!" screamed Blaze. "Just take the package!"

"Blaze, it's me."

"Hoo? I thought you were a zombie! Or something else that's super scary."

Maybe Blaze doesn't appreciate the new me, but the others will, thought Hoo. So, he continued waddling all around the Friendly Forest bumping into his friends.

"You sure are slow when you don't fly," Cubby observed.

"Did you get in a fight with a swamp creature in the Murky Marshland?" asked Hensley.

Hoo finally stopped and sobbed, "I just want to be like all of you-hoo-hoo!"

"But, Hoo," said Flora, "without you, who would watch over the forest from way up high?"

"Yeah!" added Hensley. "And blue is my favorite color!"

"So will you pleeeaaaase go back to being you?" begged Blaze.

"I sure will," answered Hoo, fluffing the muddy mess from his feathers.

Talk About It

- Why did Hoo give himself a new look?
- What did the forest friends remind Hoo about?
- What are some special things about the way God created you?

Think About It

Remember, you are created in a wonderful way. God made you to be you—and that's a really great thing!

Pray About It

Dear God,

Thank You for making me in an amazing and wonderful way. Help me be okay even when I feel a little different from others. Help me be the best me I can be!

Amen.

DAY 10

Flora and the Wheelbarrow Disaster

Your word is a lamp to guide my feet
and a light for my path.
PSALM 119:105

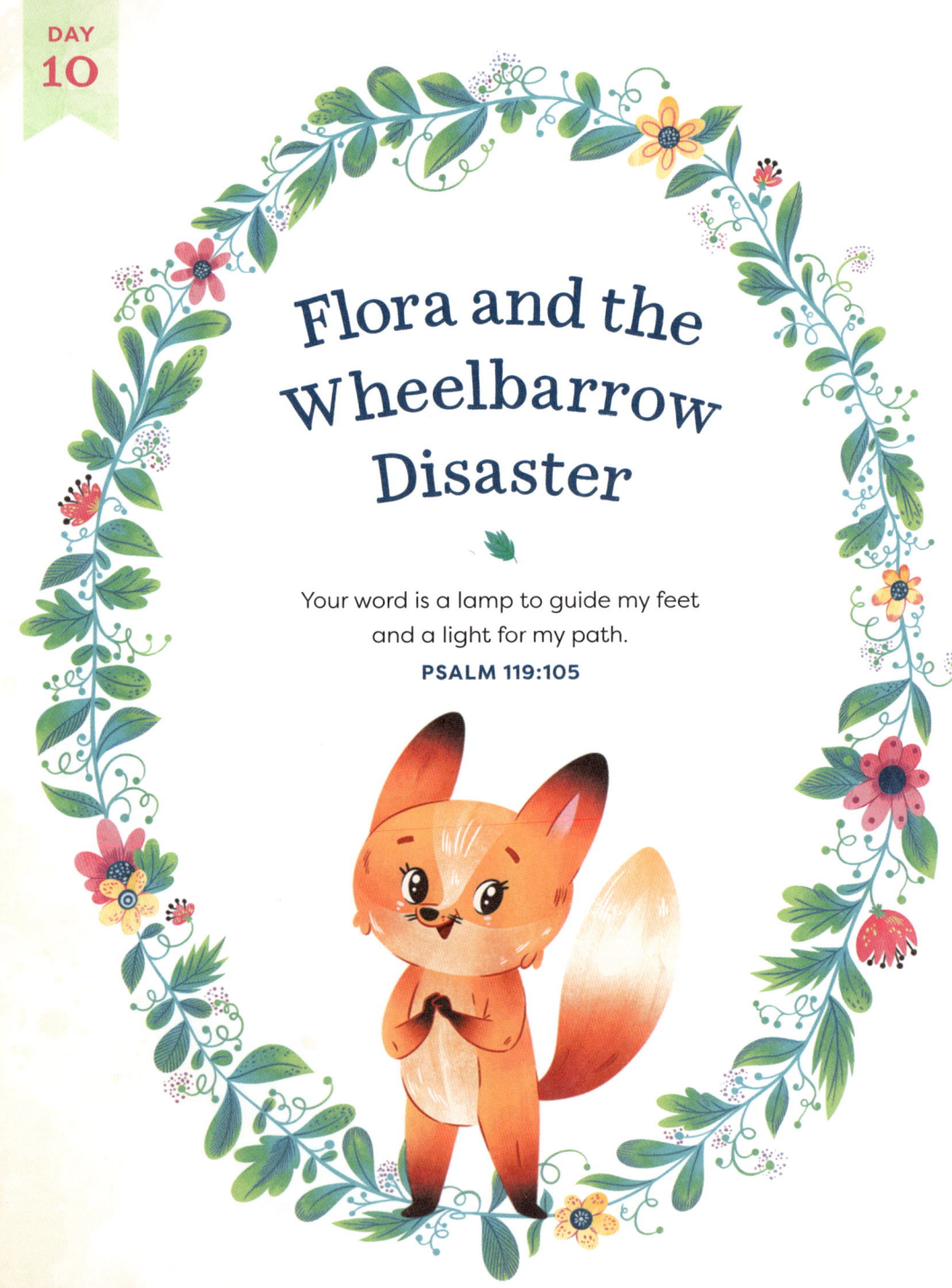

Today, Mama Fox had an important job for Flora.
"I need you to help Papa build the new wheelbarrow while I go to the store with your sister."

Flora glanced at the instruction manual Mama Fox handed her. *Are these instructions really necessary?* she wondered. *I bet I can put this together without them.*

Flora tossed the instructions to the side and got to work. She put this piece here and that piece there. A few pieces didn't quite fit, but Flora shoved them into place.

"Done!"

"Wow!" exclaimed Papa Fox as he walked outside. "Did you build this by yourself?"

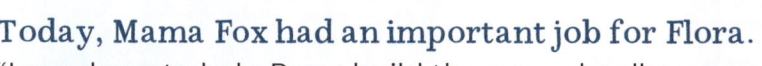

"Yep!" Flora jumped up.

"Well, let's try it out."

Papa Fox put a few logs into the wheelbarrow, and Flora started pushing. But it wouldn't move. So, she pushed harder . . . and *harder* . . . and HARDER. Suddenly Flora was catapulted into the sky! She landed with a thud inside the wheelbarrow, which quickly crumbled underneath her.

Papa Fox held up the instructions. "I'm guessing you didn't follow these?"

Flora frowned.

"It's important to follow instructions," Papa explained. "The wheelbarrow makers know how each piece fits together best."

Papa Fox opened the manual, and they read it together. Following the instructions made building the wheelbarrow *much* easier. And the wheelbarrow was *much* sturdier too!

"You know," Papa Fox said when they were finished, "because the Maker made the whole world, He knows what's best for us too! And that's why He gives us instructions about things like being kind, honest, and patient."

"I'll try to pay more attention to instructions from now on," said Flora, smiling. "Especially when they're from the Maker."

Talk About It

- Why didn't the wheelbarrow that Flora built work?
- What makes it either easy or hard for you to follow instructions?
- Why is it important to follow instructions, especially the ones God gives us?

Think About It

God gives us instructions because He loves us. He made you and knows you even better than you know yourself, so you can trust that He always knows what's best for you too!

Pray About It

Dear God,

Thank You for creating me and always wanting what's best for me. Please help me follow Your instructions with a joyful heart.

Amen.

DAY 11

Be Brave, Hensley!

God has not given us a spirit of fear and timidity, but of power, love, and self-discipline.

2 TIMOTHY 1:7

Hensley headed over to Frontier's Field on a cloudy afternoon. The forest friends were playing kickball, but when she arrived, they quickly decided to switch to hide-and-seek. After all, kickball isn't very fun for hedgehogs since they often get confused with the ball.

When it was time to hide, Hensley scurried toward a fallen tree. *This is a great spot,* she thought.

"Eighteen, nineteen, twenty!" yelled Cubby. "Ready or not . . ."

"Aaahh!" Hensley screamed, jumping out from behind the tree.

"I found you, Hensley," said Cubby. "You sure didn't make it that hard."

"No, there's something back there!" cried Hensley. "I don't know what it is—maybe a poisonous snake or a hairy, scary monster!"

"There are precisely zero poisonous snake species in the Friendly Forest," explained Hoo.

"And last I heard, monsters aren't even real," added Blaze.

"I think I need to go home," Hensley said. "I'm still just a timid baby scaredy-cat."

"Not with the Maker's help, Hensley!" said Flora. "He's always with you, even when you can't see Him. He'll help you be brave!"

Hensley said a quick prayer in her heart as she took a deep breath. "Okay, I'll stay and play—at least for a few more minutes."

Just as Hensley was about to find a new hiding spot, she noticed the cutest baby chipmunk come out from behind the fallen tree. "Aw, what a sweet little chipmunk!" Hensley gushed. "I guess I didn't need to be so scared after all. Friends, thanks for reminding me that I can be brave!"

Talk About It

- Why was Hensley feeling timid and afraid?
- What did the forest friends remind her about the Maker?
- How does it make you feel to know that God, our Maker, will help you be brave too?

Think About It

Read 2 Timothy 1:7 aloud again. Remember, God created you to be strong, powerful, and brave!

Pray About It

Dear God,

I know that You didn't create me to be timid or afraid. Please help me be brave. Thank You for loving me and giving me strength.

Amen.

DAY 12

Hoo Learns About Gratitude

Be thankful in all circumstances, for this is God's will for you who belong to Christ Jesus.

1 THESSALONIANS 5:18

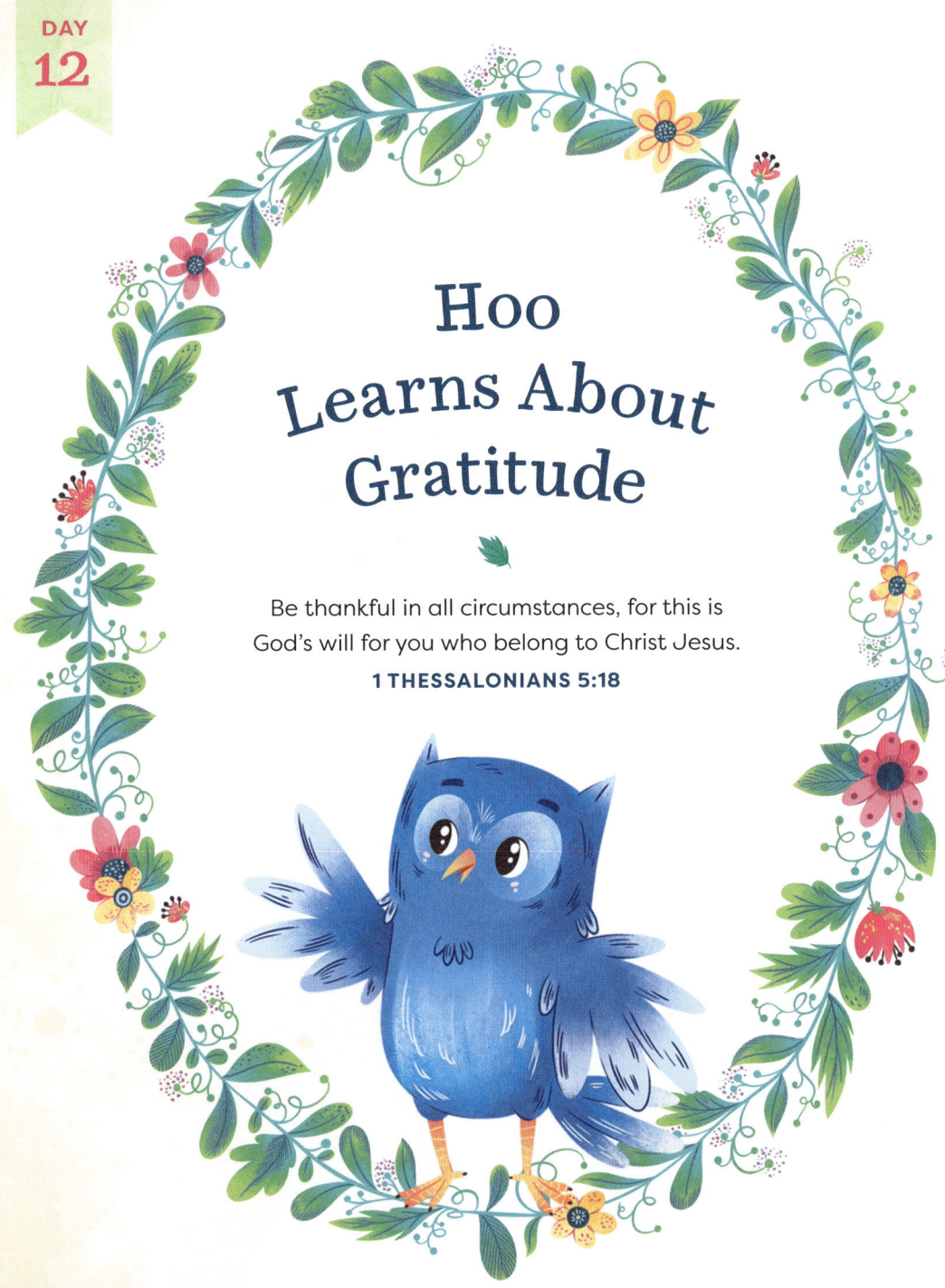

Hoo huffed and puffed around the half-unpacked boxes. He'd spent the last three nights collecting leftover wood scraps from the Rebuild and Restore Team. His plan to use the wood to divide the bedroom he shared with his brother into two separate rooms had seemed flawless. But his parents said no.

"But, Mom, Ollie is *always* making a mess," Hoo argued. "We didn't have to share a room at our old house."

"Hoo," said Mama Owl, "things in life can't always be exactly how we want them. Try to have an attitude of gratitude."

"Okay," Hoo grumbled, not sure if he'd ever find anything to be thankful for. He decided to escape to Blaze's house.

Hoo was welcomed into the Bunny residence. With Blaze plus all his ten brothers and twelve sisters hanging out in their shared bedroom, it sure was loud!

"Whoa!" Hoo exclaimed. "How do you-hoo get any sleep?"

"We don't really. But we play games and make up hip-hopping dance moves together!" Blaze showed off a new hop combo. "It's super-de-duper fun!"

Hoo's eyes grew extra wide. He was suddenly very grateful he had to share a bedroom with only his *one* brother.

As Hoo flew back toward his tree, he saw Hensley playing outside. "Hi, Hoo! Wanna play with me?" Hensley called out.

It sure is fun living right next door to one of my best friends, Hoo thought as he swooped down to join her. Another thing to be grateful for!

The next morning, the sun peeked through the branches. Delicious smells wafted into Hoo's bedroom window from Grammy's Bakery. Hoo smiled and closed his sleepy eyes. "Maybe having an attitude of gratitude isn't so hard after all."

Talk About It

- What was Hoo being ungrateful about?
- How can we have an attitude of gratitude toward God and others?
- What are five things you're thankful for right now?

Think About It

God gives us so much, like friends and family and food to eat. Turn your list of five things from the last question into a prayer by thanking God for all He's given you!

Pray About It

Dear God,

Thank You for all the awesome things You've given me. Please help me have an attitude of gratitude by being thankful for what I have.

Amen.

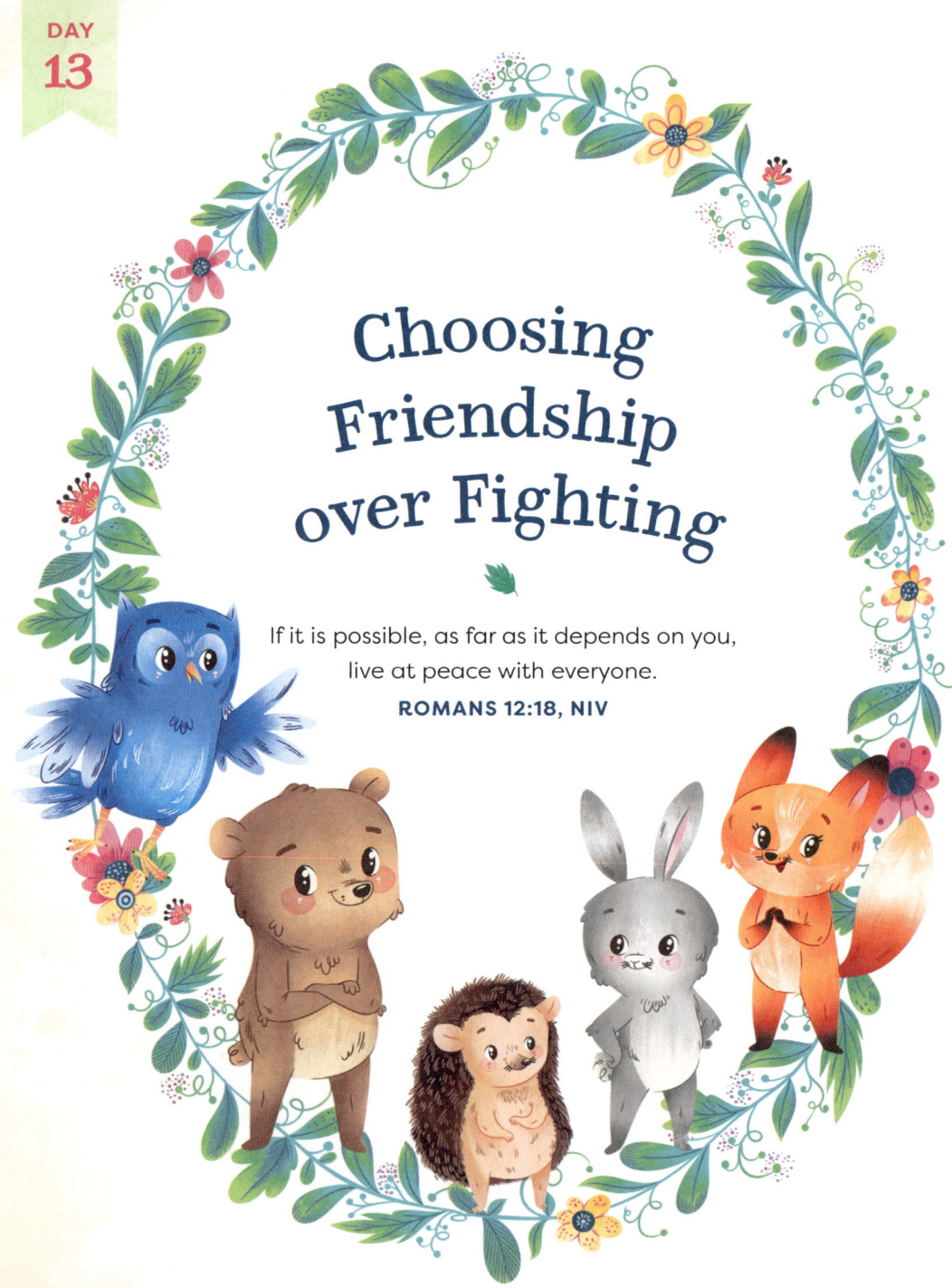

DAY 13

Choosing Friendship over Fighting

If it is possible, as far as it depends on you,
live at peace with everyone.

ROMANS 12:18, NIV

The Friendly Forest rebuilding efforts were moving along well—so well, in fact, that the friends could take a bit of a break. They decided to build their very own tree fort with the wood scraps Hoo had collected!

But they hadn't even picked up a hammer yet when the disagreements started.

"We'll use all this space for our strategizing sessions," said Hoo. "We need to be sure the forest is fully prepared for winter."

"No, I want a play space!" said Blaze.

"That seems selfish," Hoo responded.

"I'm with Blaze," said Hensley. "I want a place to play. We're still kids after all."

"But the forest needs us," argued Cubby.

It was two against two. The arguing continued, and hurtful words were exchanged.

"Stop fighting!" Flora finally interrupted. "We can figure this out."

It was too late. Cubby and Hoo stomped and flew off one way, and Hensley and Blaze went the other.

Flora sighed and headed toward Grammy's Bakery. While waiting for her evening snack, she prayed, "Dear Maker, please help my friends learn to live in peace. Amen."

A few minutes later, Cubby and Hoo slipped into the bakery. Blaze and Hensley followed shortly after, and Flora nudged the four of them toward each other.

"We're sorry," Cubby and Hoo apologized.

"So are we," said Hensley and Blaze.

As the friends filled their bellies, Flora helped them listen to each other and respond respectfully. "See," said Flora, "choosing peace can be easier than it seems!"

Talk About It

- What were the forest friends arguing about?
- It's fine to disagree about things, but how can we choose friendship over fighting?
- Why do you think God wants people to get along and live in peace?

Think About It

While we might not always agree with our friends or family members, we can still listen and choose to use kind words. Remember, God wants us to live in peace with others!

Pray About It

Dear God,

Please help me get along with the people around me. Help me be a good listener and share my thoughts in a respectful way.

Amen.

DAY
14

Hensley (Finally) Asks for Help

Two people are better than one.
They get more done by working together.

ECCLESIASTES 4:9, ICB

"**The tree fort is almost done!**" said Cubby. "I'm glad we decided to make one space that can be used for everything."

"Yeah! We can play here, and we can straighter-eyes here too!" shouted Blaze.

"Strategize," Hoo corrected.

"Oh, that's right. Splatter-gize."

"Anyway, we should probably see how Hensley is doing," Cubby chimed in.

Even though they had offered to help, Hensley had insisted on doing the painting all by herself.

"It's not ready yet!" Hensley shouted when she heard her friends coming.

"Okay," Cubby replied. "Are you sure you don't need help?"

"I've got this!" said Hensley.

But she had just as much paint on herself as the walls did—maybe more. There were splatters on the ceiling and an entire can of paint spilled all over the floor. Hensley couldn't remember why she was so determined to do this on her own.

"Actually," she called down, "a little help might be nice!"

"Be right there!" her friends responded.

"Whoa!" exclaimed Blaze. "Did the paint cans explode?"

"Not exactly . . ." Hensley felt a bit embarrassed, but her friends immediately got to work.

Cubby carried the heavy paint cans while Hoo flew in and out with ease tackling the window trim. Blaze touched up the corners and of course was done in a flash.

Things were moving along smoothly, but Hensley knew they needed one more friend to come if they wanted to finish the work by bedtime . . .

"Hey, guys! I'll be right back," she announced. "I'm going to find Flora to help us too!"

Talk About It

- What was Hensley trying to do all on her own?
- When is the last time you've asked others for help?
- What could God help you with today?

Think About It

God will help us, and He gives us other people who can support us too. So, don't be afraid to ask for help. We're not meant to do life all on our own!

Pray About It

Dear God,

Thank You for giving me other people in my life so I don't have to do everything on my own. And thank You for always being there to help me love You and love others as well!

Amen.

DAY 15

Left Out or Invited In

Accept one another, then, just as Christ accepted you, in order to bring praise to God.

ROMANS 15:7, NIV

The tree fort was finally finished! The forest friends were excited to have an evening filled with fun and games together.

"What ah you doing up there?" Flora's little sister, Fiona, called to the friends, who had just settled into their new space.

"Don't answer," said Flora. "Fiona has been bugging me all day."

A few minutes later, Fiona popped her head through the window. "Oh, you *are* he-ew! I didn't he-ew anything, so I thought you wuh playing somewhere else. But then I thought maybe you all lost your voices and couldn't answ-ew. Or that maybe the twee fort was soundproof and you didn't he-ew me, or—"

"Yep, we're here, Fiona," Flora interrupted. "But we're playing paws and claws, and you don't know that game. So you can just go home."

"We can teach her the rules!" exclaimed Cubby.

Hoo motioned for Fiona to come in. "We'll show you what to do-hoo-hoo."

Flora rolled her eyes as her friends explained the game to her sister. But as she watched Fiona and saw how excited she was, Flora's heart began to soften. Even though Fiona was a little annoying at times, she really was sweet too. Plus, she didn't have a great group of friends to play with like Flora did.

"I fow-get what to do now," said Fiona.

"I'll help you." Flora hurried to her sister's side. "You're really getting the hang of this," she commented. "Maybe you can play with us more often."

Fiona beamed and hopped up to give her big sis a hug. "Thanks, Flo-wah!"

Talk About It

- What happened between Flora and her sister, Fiona?
- Why do you think God wants us to invite others in instead of leaving people out?
- How can you show kindness by including someone who might get left out a lot?

Think About It

It can be fine to do things on our own or with certain friends at times, but remember to include others when you can. And guess what? God wants to welcome everyone, including you, into His big family!

Pray About It

Dear God,

Please help me include others more instead of leaving them out. Thank You for inviting me to be part of Your big, awesome family!

Amen.

DAY 16

Blaze Learns About Self-Control

A person without self-control
is like a city with broken-down walls.
PROVERBS 25:28

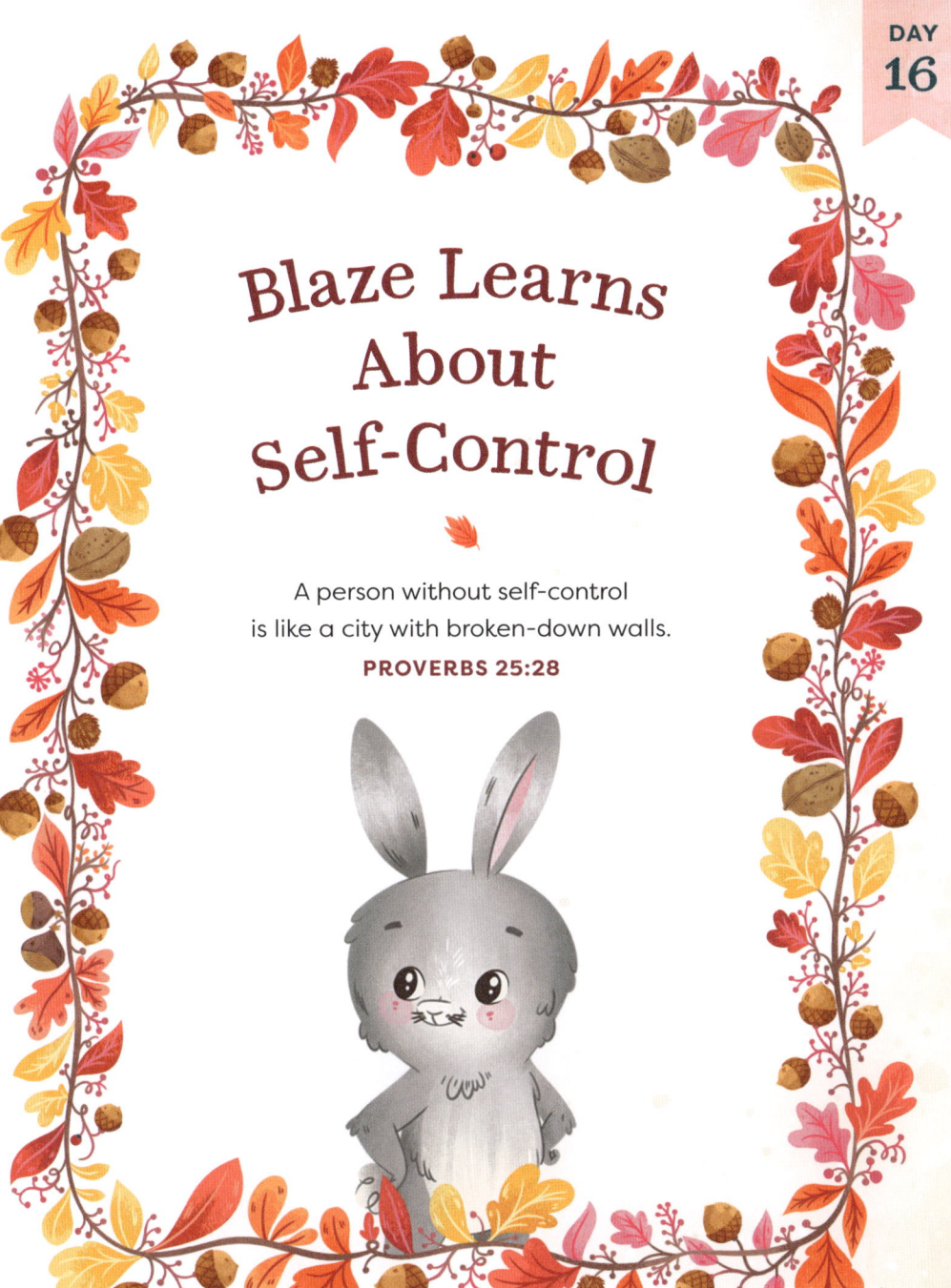

Blaze sped over to Grammy's Bakery. "Are those berry blast cookies?" he asked as drool began to drip from his mouth.

"They sure are!" said Grammy. "We're making a whole bunch to celebrate. The Rebuild and Restore Team has almost finished fixing the North Bridge! And it looks like *all* the repairs in the forest will be done before winter."

"Yippee! This means we don't have to move!" said Blaze.

"Yep!" said Grammy Bear. "Here's a box of cookies to share with your family."

Blaze raced away to finish his deliveries. *They will be so excited,* he thought.

But as he zoomed here and there, his tummy started grumbling. So Blaze ate a cookie. "Mmm. That was delightfully delicious. Maybe just one more . . ."

Half an hour later, Blaze looked into the box and saw a few broken cookie pieces and some crumbs. He had eaten the whole box!

Just then, Flora and Hensley scampered by.

"Are you okay, Blaze?" Hensley asked.

"I don't feel good," said Blaze. Between grunts and groans he explained what had happened. "I

didn't *mean* to eat them all. They were just *so* good!"

"It sounds like you could use some self-control," said Flora.

"What's that?" asked Blaze.

"It's having control over the things you say or do. It keeps you from hurting others when you're angry. And it's what helps you eat one cookie instead of two . . . or twenty-five."

"I definitely need some self-control," moaned Blaze. "And now I also need someone to help me move."

So, Flora and Hensley rolled their funny bunny friend all the way home.

Talk About It

- What does it mean to use self-control?
- When is a time you've struggled to use self-control?
- Why does God want us to have self-control?

Think About It

Having self-control isn't always easy (even for grown-ups!), but you can ask God to show you how. He's always willing to help!

Pray About It

Dear God,

Please help me control my words and actions in a way that honors You. You know what's best for me, and I need Your help to use self-control.

Amen.

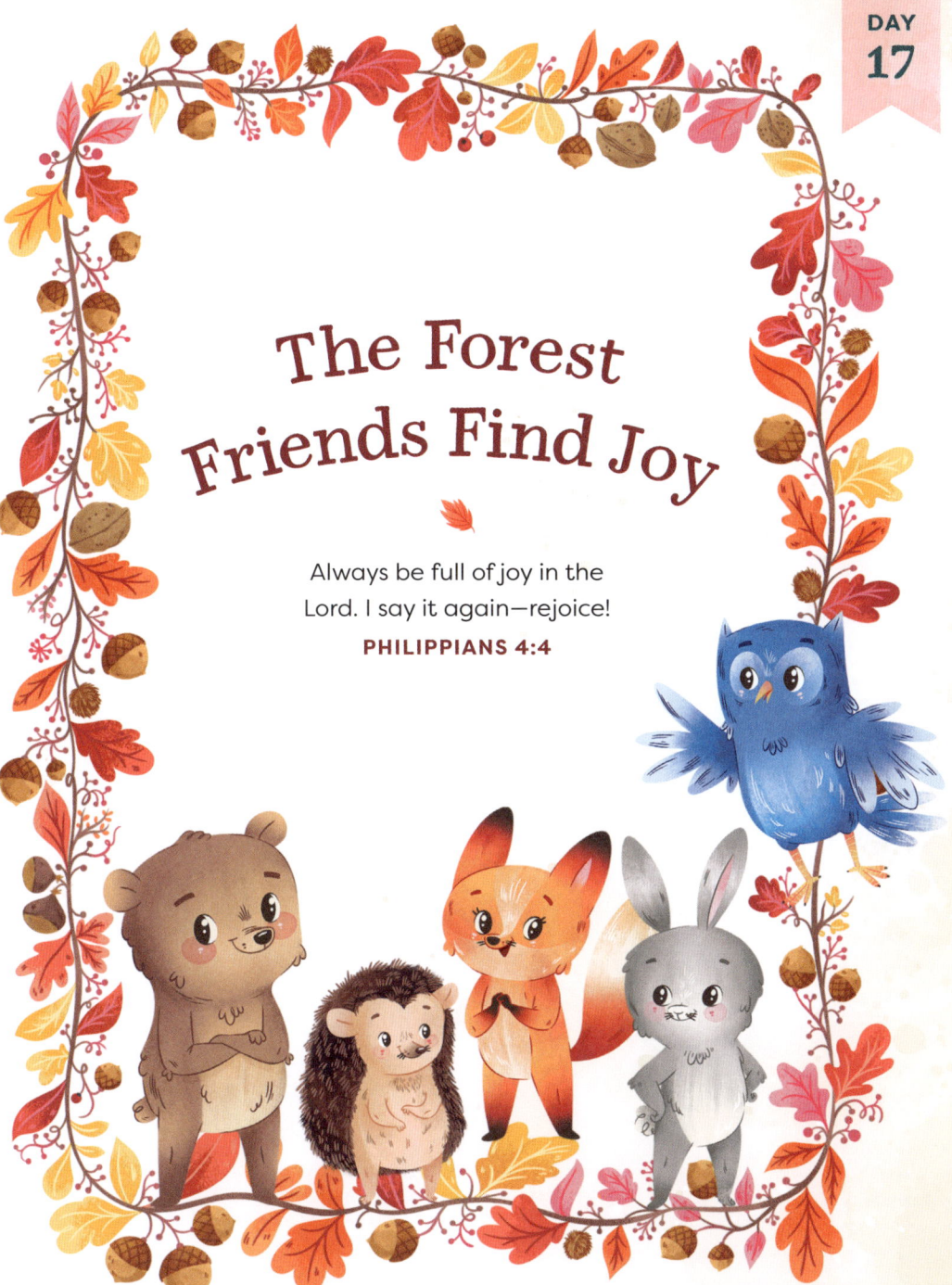

DAY 17

The Forest Friends Find Joy

Always be full of joy in the Lord. I say it again—rejoice!

PHILIPPIANS 4:4

Just when the forest friends thought the worst was behind them, another storm blew through the Friendly Forest. It knocked down many more trees, buried den doors underneath heavy brush, and washed away the newly restored trails. It looked like the day after the first storm all over again.

"I can't believe it!" cried Hensley.

"All our hard work was for nothing," said Cubby.

"Now we'll *definitely* have to leave the forest!" Hoo boo-hooed.

"How could the Maker let this happen?" asked Flora.

"We don't always understand the Maker's ways," said Grammy. "But because of His love for us, there's always something to be joyful about."

The forest friends looked at Grammy in surprise. How could anyone have joy right now?

"The Maker can bring good from hard, sad, and even downright bad things," Grammy continued. "So, we can have joy even in the worst times! Let's all go around and say one thing we're grateful to the Maker for. I'll start. I'm thankful for each one of you!"

After a short pause, Hensley added, "I'm thankful that the Maker kept us all safe."

One by one, they each shared one thing they were thankful for.

Then it was Blaze's turn. "I'm thankful that our tree fort is still standing . . . and that I feel better after eating all those cookies yesterday!"

Everyone started laughing. Who would have thought joy could be found on a day like this?

Talk About It

- Why were the forest friends sad at first in today's story?
- What did Grammy say that God can do with hard or bad things that happen?
- Read Philippians 4:4 again. How can we always have joy?

Think About It

God created us to have fun and be joyful. We can have joy no matter what because of what Jesus did for us by dying on the cross and coming back to life!

Pray About It

Dear God,

Thank You for loving me and sending Jesus for me. Help me remember that because of Jesus, I can have joy no matter what!

Amen.

DAY 18

The Forest Friends Serve Others

In everything I did, I showed you that we must work hard and help the weak. We must remember the words of the Lord Jesus. He said, "It is more blessed to give than to receive."

ACTS 20:35, NIRV

"Papa, I'm so glad you're home!" Hensley shouted.

"Me too," said Papa Hedgehog. "I wish I could stay longer, but I'll need to go back to the Western Woodland with more food in a couple of days."

"But, Papa, we have so much to do here in the Friendly Forest. Who will help us?"

"The second storm wiped out nearly all the food sources for the creatures in the Western Woodland," Papa said. "At least we have enough food for the next few weeks."

Hensley thought about what her dad said. Then she ran off to find Flora and tell her what was going on in the Western Woodland. "Do you think we can help?"

Flora was immediately on board and had an idea. She shared her plan with Hensley, and the two hurried off to find the rest of their friends. Soon they were all collecting berries, honey, and more goodies!

The next day, the forest friends came together and admired their hard work: a wagon piled high with food for the creatures of the Western Woodland. "This is sure to help," said Hensley. "My dad is so grateful too. But wait, where's Blaze?"

Blaze raced toward the group. "I got some berry blast cookies to add! And guess what? I didn't even eat any!"

"Hey, how about we pray for the animals in the Western Woodland?" Hensley said.

So, the group bowed their fuzzy and feathery heads and prayed for these faraway friends.

Talk About It

- How did the forest friends serve the creatures in the Western Woodland?
- What are some ways that Jesus served others while He was here on earth? (If you need a couple of ideas, read Matthew 14:13–21 and John 13:1–17.)
- What are some ways that you could serve others?

Think About It

Jesus gave amazing examples of what it looks like to serve others while He was here on earth. Jesus's ultimate act of service for the whole world was when He gave His life for us!

Pray About It

Dear God,

Thank You for sending Jesus, who gave His life to save us from our sins. Please help me serve others and show people Jesus's love. I love You.

Amen.

DAY 19

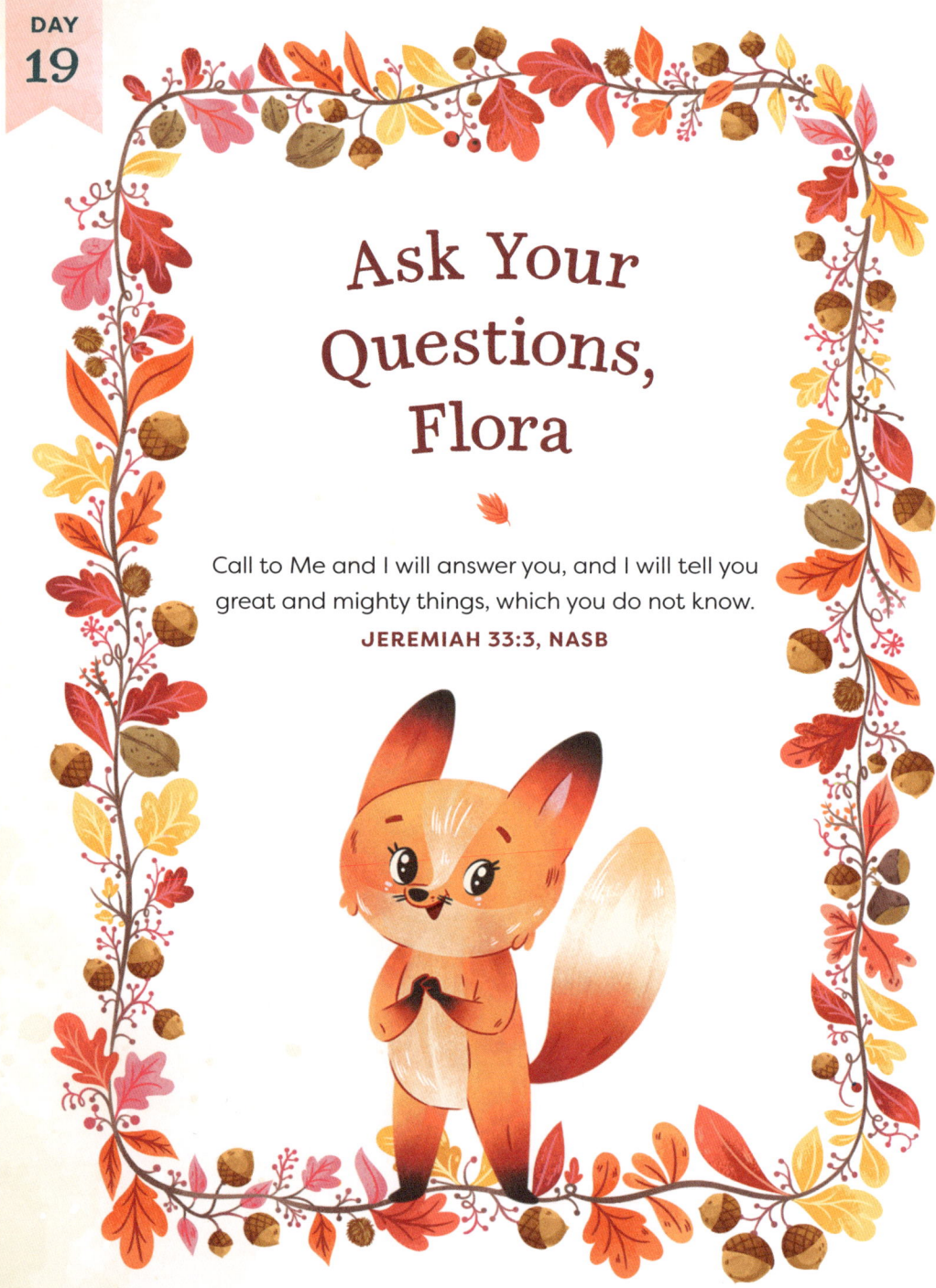

Ask Your Questions, Flora

Call to Me and I will answer you, and I will tell you great and mighty things, which you do not know.

JEREMIAH 33:3, NASB

It was just a dream, **Flora said** to herself. *It was just a really bad dream.*

Flora slipped quietly into the kitchen and saw Papa Fox making breakfast. "Want some pancakes, Flora?"

"They're weally good!" exclaimed her sister, Fiona.

Normally Flora would giggle at the sight of sticky syrup all over Fiona's orange fur, but instead she just said, "I'm sure they are, but I'm not hungry."

Flora headed back into her room and plopped on her bed. *Why did I have such a scary dream?* she wondered. She grabbed her journal and tried writing. That usually helped her feel better, but it didn't this time. She felt like she was stuck.

As she closed her journal, her dad walked in and asked, "Flora, are you sure you're okay?"

Flora broke down in tears. "Oh, Papa, it was terrible. I had a dream that there was a third storm and that the entire Friendly Forest just disappeared. I kept asking other animals what was going on, but no one would answer me. Why would I have a dream like that?"

"We don't always know what our dreams mean," Papa Fox replied. "But it sounds like you might have some unanswered questions about what will happen if we need to leave the Friendly Forest."

"I do have questions," said Flora. "A lot of them."

"All right, my dear," said Papa Fox. "I'm listening."

So, Flora and Papa Fox spent the rest of the morning talking through all sorts of things. Even though her dad didn't have all the answers, Flora was really glad she had someone willing to listen to all her questions.

Talk About It

- What was Flora upset about in the story?
- Who do you like to talk to if you have questions?
- What is a question you have about God?

Think About It

Whenever you have questions, you can ask others who love Jesus, search for what the Bible says about them, or go directly to God through prayer. We might not get answers to all our questions here on earth. But we can trust that God knows what's true and that He's always watching over us!

Pray About It

Dear God,

Thank You for giving me a mind that can think and ask questions. As I look for answers, please show Your truth to me. And help me trust You, even when I don't have the answers.

Amen.

DAY 20

Blaze Needs to Practice Patience

Be patient, brothers and sisters, until the coming of the Lord. The farmer waits for the precious produce of the soil, being patient about it, until it gets the early and late rains.

JAMES 5:7, NASB

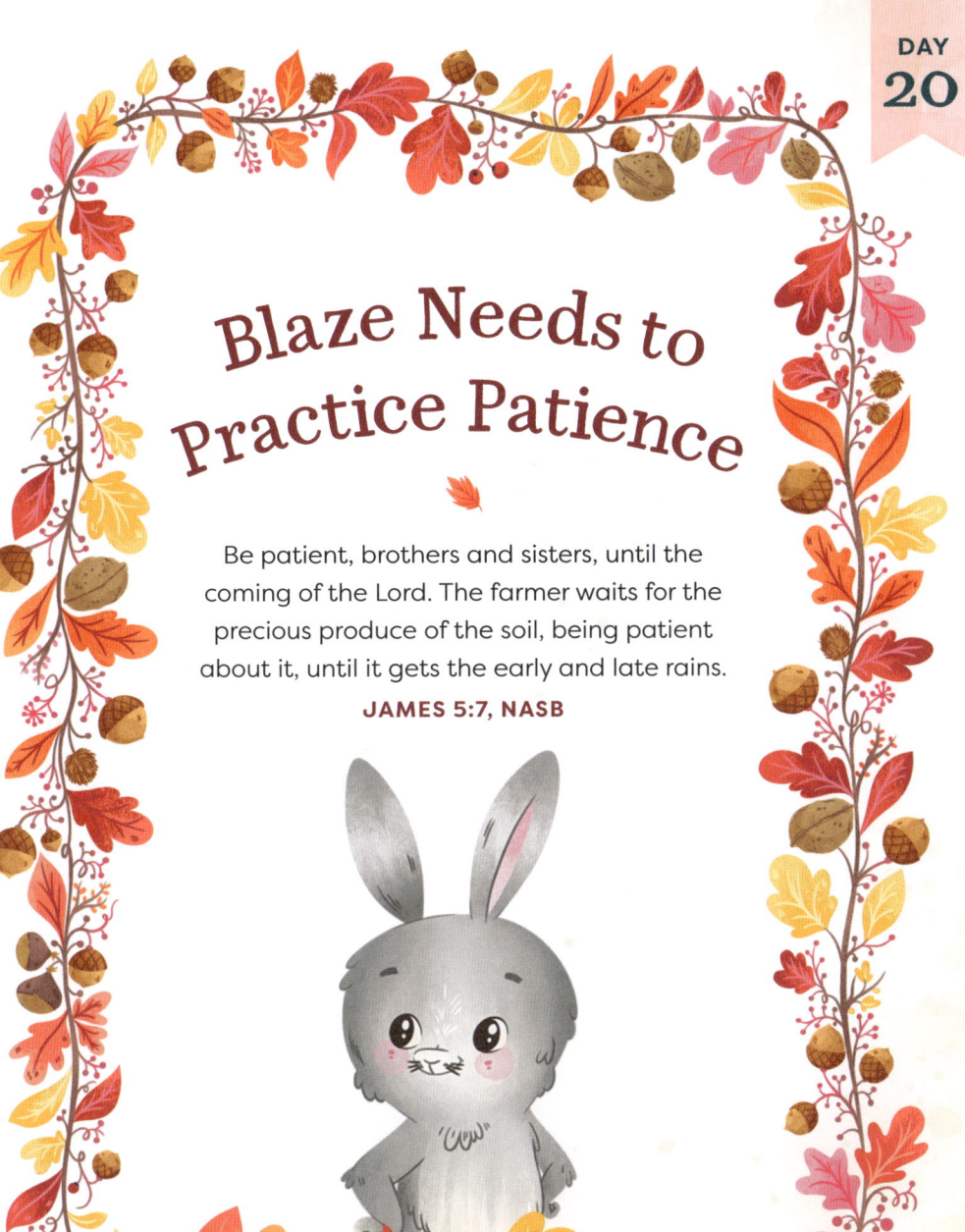

"**How long does it take vegetables** to grow?" Blaze asked Cubby as the two friends finished planting seeds in the winter garden.

"It'll be a while, buddy," Cubby said as he turned to go home.

There's got to be a way to speed this up, Blaze thought. *I know! I'll do a super-speedy dance.*

So, Blaze performed his best hip-hoppity moves. But the vegetables didn't grow a bit.

What next? Blaze remembered some words from Grammy Bear: "*Sometimes the best way to grow is to get good rest and take it slow.*"

"Hmm . . . slow. Ooh, I know!" Blaze said as he raced off.

He returned to the garden with a pile of snails. But they began eating the seeds!

As Blaze grabbed every snail, he remembered something Hensley had said: "*It can feel scary trying things that are new, but after you do, you will notice you grew!*"

"Something new!" exclaimed Blaze. "I've never stood on my head."

A few minutes into Blaze's headstand, Flora walked by, giggling. "Blaze, what are you doing?"

"I'm trying something new to help the seeds grow speedy fast!"

"How about we just give them some water?" suggested Flora.

"Is that what helps them grow?" asked Blaze.

"Yes, but we'll still need to be patient."

"I guess I'm out of tricks anyway," said Blaze. "I'll try this patience thing."

So, after a sprinkle of water, the two friends headed toward home.

"I can't wait to tell my brothers and sisters all about this," said Blaze. "Or maybe I *can* wait—at least a few minutes."

Talk About It

- What was Blaze not-so-patiently waiting for?
- Why do you think God wants us to be patient?
- What are some things that are hard for you to wait for?

Think About It

Choosing to be patient can be really hard! But did you know that God will help you be patient? God is the most patient of all, and He wants to help us wait well too.

Pray About It

Dear God,

Please help me be patient when I'm waiting for something. Thank You for waiting patiently for me and helping me continue to become more like You.

Amen.

Cubby Tells the Truth

The LORD detests lying lips,
but he delights in those who tell the truth.

PROVERBS 12:22

"**Cubby, can you go to the bakery and** help me unpack the new serving plates I got?" asked Grammy Bear.

"I sure can!" he answered.

Once there, Cubby decided to tidy up the bakery before unpacking the plates. He had just finished and was turning to put the mop away when—*whoosh!*—he slipped on the wet floor. While trying to regain his balance, he accidentally bumped the box of plates. The box slid off the countertop and landed on the floor with a great big crash!

"Noooooo!" yelled Cubby.

Moments after he had cleaned up the shattered mess, Grammy walked in.

"Hi, Grammy! Instead of your new plates, w-w-why don't you use these blue plates?" Cubby's left ear began to twitch. "They match your blueberry pie."

"I'd really like to use my new plates. Where are they?" asked Grammy.

"Umm . . ."

"Cubby, what is happening to your ear? It's twitching like Blaze after he's had too many cookies!"

"I . . . uh . . ."

"Cubby, please tell me where my new plates are."

Cubby took a deep breath. "I slipped and bumped into your plates. They're all broken, and I'm really sorry!"

"Oh, it's all right," said Grammy. "They're only plates after all. I'm glad you chose to tell the truth. The Maker wants us to always be truthful! It's one of the most important things we can do to have good relationships."

Cubby's ear stopped twitching, and he smiled at Grammy. "Do you want me to set out the blue plates for tonight?"

"Yes, Cubby. That would be lovely."

Talk About It

- Why do you think Cubby was nervous to tell the truth?
- How can hiding the truth hurt our relationships with others?
- Why does God want us to tell the truth all the time, not just sometimes?

Think About It

Remember, God wants us to be people who always tell the truth! When we're truthful, we can grow strong, good relationships and become worthy of trust.

Pray About It

Dear God,

Thank You for loving me even when I make mistakes. Please help me tell the truth so I can have a good relationship with You and with others.

Amen.

DAY 22

Hoo's Forgiveness Dilemma

Be kind and tender to one another. Forgive one another, just as God forgave you because of what Christ has done.

EPHESIANS 4:32, NIRV

A loud commotion woke Hoo from his sleep.
He peeked his head out to see what was going on.

"There he is!" a squirrel shouted.

"He looks even weirder than I imagined!" exclaimed another squirrel, laughing.

"Like a creature from the Murky Marshland!" said the first squirrel as they ran off.

Hoo tried to go back to sleep, but his heart was hurting. He finally rolled out of bed to find his friends outside. He was too sad to play and instead told them what the squirrels had said about him.

"What if we got those squirrels back by playing a trick on them?" suggested Blaze.

"Hmm . . . maybe," said Hoo.

"Or you could choose to forgive them," suggested Cubby.

"Forgive them? But they were so mean," said Blaze as the friends saw the two squirrels heading toward them. "Now's your chance, Hoo! Pretend . . . pretend that you're going to eat them! Then you can forgive later if you want."

But before Hoo could even decide what to do, the squirrels asked if they could play tag with the forest friends. Cubby and Blaze both looked at Hoo to see how he'd respond.

He knew playing a mean trick might feel good for a moment. But he didn't want the squirrels to feel as bad as they had made him feel.

"Hey, squirrels," Hoo finally said, "what you said earlier really hurt my feelings. But I forgive you, and you can play with us."

"We're sorry, Hoo," the squirrels said. "Thanks for forgiving us."

"Forgiving is what real friends do-hoo-hoo!"

Talk About It

- Why was Hoo upset in the story?
- What does it mean to forgive someone?
- Why do you think God wants us to forgive others?

Think About It

In a way, forgiving is just as much for you as it is for the other person because holding grudges can actually hurt you. So, ask God to help you forgive. When we follow Jesus, He forgives us and wants us to forgive others too!

Pray About It

Dear God,

Thank You for sending Jesus to die on the cross and rise again so that I could be forgiven. Please help me forgive others just like You forgive.

Amen.

DAY 23

What Will Flora Follow?

Don't copy the behavior and customs of this world, but let God transform you into a new person by changing the way you think.

ROMANS 12:2

"**Flora, what's on your head?**" asked Hensley.

"I saw some of the fox teens wearing them yesterday," answered Flora. "It's a Fashion Fox hat, the latest trend."

"It mostly looks like you're just wearing a giant bucket on your head, but okay!" said Hensley. "Can you even see?"

"Kind of," said Flora, facing the opposite direction. "Want to walk to the cleanup day together?"

Flora chattered away as Hensley led the two friends along the trail. "My mom said I should be more concerned with helping the forest than with fashion," Flora admitted. "But who said you can't be helpful and stylish at the same time?" A few seconds later, Flora tripped over a tree stump.

"Your mom might have a point," said Hensley.

Hensley doesn't understand fashion either, Flora thought.

Flora continued toward the Babbling Brook, rake in paw. She was ready to work. When she got to the brook, she noticed what appeared to be a big pile of leaves. Flora began raking the pile, but the leaves wouldn't move!

"Thanks for the fur raking, Flora, but I think it'd be best if you raked the leaves instead," said Cubby.

"Oops!" said Flora. She backed away, tripped on another tree stump, and tumbled right into the Babbling Brook with a splash. Sopping wet, she limped out.

"Maybe I don't need to follow *all* the trends," said Flora. She took off her Fashion Fox hat and began to fill it up with leaves and rocks. "This does make a great bucket, though!"

Talk About It

- Why do you think Flora wanted to copy or conform to what she saw the older foxes doing?
- Can you think of a time when you copied something or someone and it turned out to be a not-so-good choice?
- Why does God want us to follow Jesus instead of following the ways of the world?

Think About It

There are a lot of people we could follow—some good and some bad—but Jesus is the best leader ever! When we follow Him, we're not conforming to the ways of the world; instead, we're transforming into the people God created us to be!

Pray About It

Dear God,

Thank You for giving us Jesus as the best example to follow. Please help me become more like Jesus every single day.

Amen.

DAY 24

Hensley Does the Next Right Thing

He has shown you, O mortal, what is good.
And what does the Lord require of you?
To act justly and to love mercy
and to walk humbly with your God.

MICAH 6:8, NIV

On her way to Grammy's Bakery, Hensley ran into a big branch lying in the middle of Critter Crossing. She looked around. The forest was still a mess, and winter was on its way. *Will the forest be cleaned up in time?* she wondered.

Hensley began to shake, partly from the chill in the air and partly from the fear taking over her thoughts. She'd been practicing taking deep breaths in moments like this, and she took one now. Then she noticed a few little mice scamper along the ground. Each moved a rock that was barely bigger than a pebble. They kept moving one tiny rock at a time, creating a guideline for small critters along the path.

Those mice don't seem stressed or fearful, Hensley thought. *They are just doing the next right thing.*

Hensley's dad often talked about the importance of doing the next right thing. He said it could be saying a prayer, sitting with a friend, or even eating a sandwich.

Although Hensley wished her dad were by her side right then to tell her what to do, she knew she could figure this out on her own. So, what was her next right thing?

The big branch she had run into caught her eye again. It was lying right in the middle of the trail.

I could walk around it . . . or I could help move it, she said to herself. Then, using all her strength, she pulled the heavy branch off the trail.

"There." She dusted off her paws. "And now on to the next right thing."

Talk About It

- What did Hensley learn from watching the mice?
- What are some other good "next right things" Hensley might do?
- Think of a challenging situation in your life right now. What next right thing could you do?

Think About It

God gives us the Bible as a tool to help us figure out our next right thing. You can also ask God to help guide you through prayer or the wisdom of others around you. He will help you do the next right thing when you trust in Him!

Pray About It

Dear God,

Please help me do the next right thing, whether it seems small and unimportant or big and scary. I know You'll always be there to guide me and love me.

Amen.

DAY 25

You Can Be Kind, Cubby

Love is patient and kind. Love is not jealous or boastful or proud or rude.

1 CORINTHIANS 13:4–5

"Good morning, Frank!"
Cubby waved at his new neighbor. Frank just grunted and turned to go back inside. This was the third time Frank had all but ignored Cubby's attempts to say hello.

I'm done being nice to that guy, Cubby thought.

"My new neighbor is so rude," said Cubby as he and Blaze helped make lunches for the Rebuild and Restore Team.

"But we live in the Friendly Forest," said Blaze. "Isn't it illegal to be rude here?"

"You'd think we were in the Murky Marshland," replied Cubby, rolling his eyes.

Blaze grabbed the stack of lunches. "I'm hopping out to deliver these, but I hope your neighbor learns how to be nice!"

A few minutes later, Grammy walked in with a basket of fresh berries and began gathering the remaining ingredients for her famous blueberry pie.

"Who's the pie for?" asked Cubby.

"It's for our new neighbor," answered Grammy.

"Why? He's certainly not acting very neighborly toward us."

"Frank had to leave the Tall Timberland, the place he'd always called home," said Grammy. "That doesn't excuse his behavior, but can you imagine how that might feel?"

Cubby *could* imagine. In fact, he'd been imagining that very thing ever since the first storm blew through the Friendly Forest. "That would be terrible," said Cubby.

"None of us deserve the love we get from the Maker," said Grammy. "But He loves us anyway."

Cubby knew that Grammy was right. "Grammy, I'll help make the pie. Frank might not deserve it, but like you always say, we're sent to love."

Talk About It

- Why didn't Cubby want to show kindness to the new neighbor at first?
- Read 1 Corinthians 13:4–5 again. What does it say that love is and isn't?
- How can you show love and kindness to someone this week?

Think About It

We've all been unkind at one time or another, but God loves us and shows us kindness anyway! God will help us show kindness to others too.

Pray About It

Dear God,

Thank You for showing me kindness and loving me, even when I don't deserve it. Please help me show kindness to those around me.

Amen.

DAY 26

Wise Up, Blaze!

If any of you needs wisdom, you should ask God for it. He will give it to you. God gives freely to everyone and doesn't find fault.

JAMES 1:5, NIRV

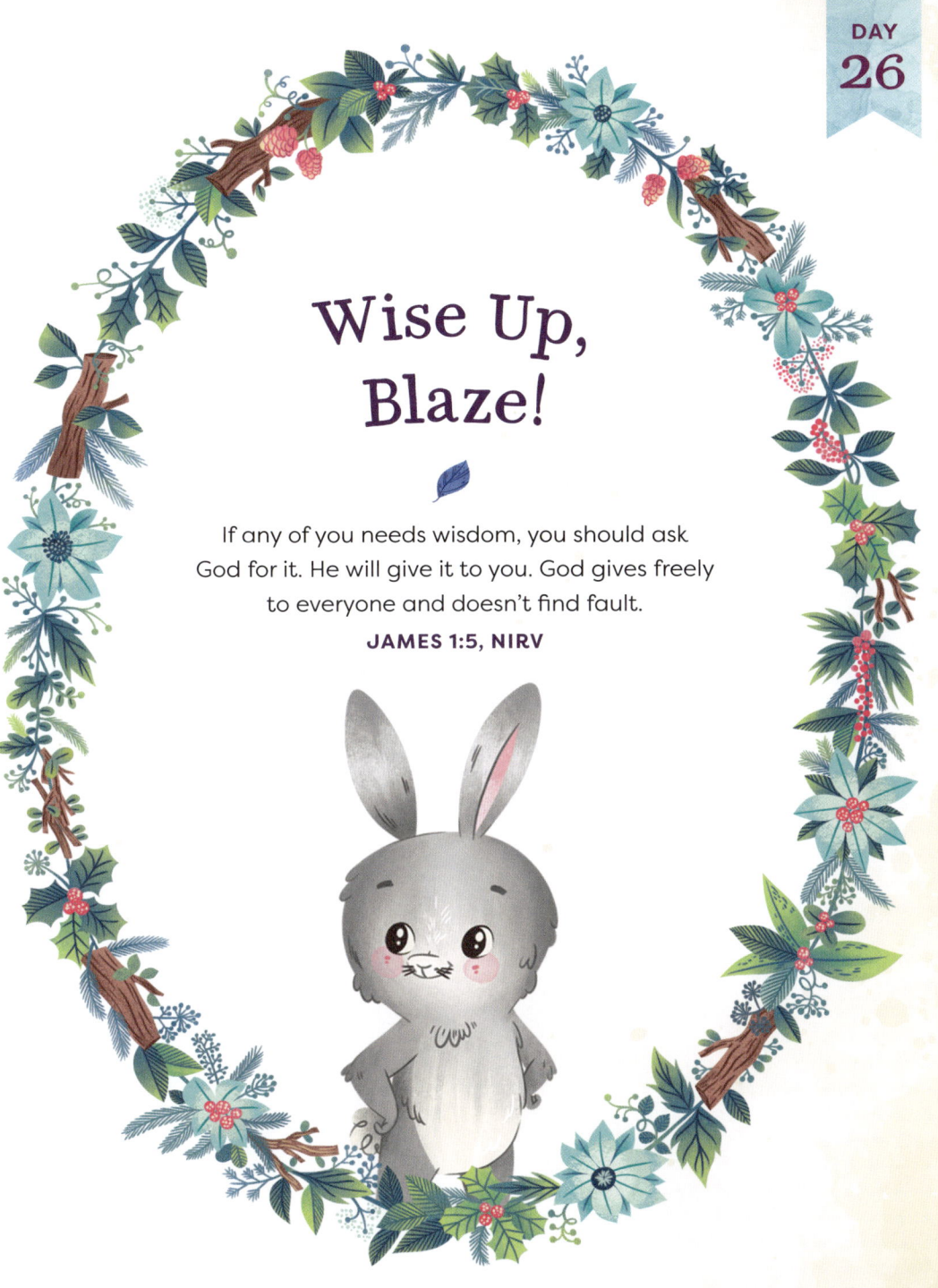

"Hoo, can you teach me how to fly?" asked Blaze one afternoon. "Imagine everything I could do to help the Friendly Forest if I could hop, race, *and* fly!"

"Flying is a skill that can't be taught," said Hoo. "But . . . maybe we could make you some sort of contraption to help you fly."

"That'd be flip-flying-fantastic!"

So, Blaze and Hoo got to work. They measured, cut, taped, and sewed until they had what slightly resembled a pair of wings.

"Now," said Hoo, "if you're able to get to a speed of exactly 270 miles per hour and jump up at an angle of 72.5 degrees, you might hit the perfect velocity for flying."

"Super-de-duper!" Blaze shouted.

Blaze strapped the wings on tight. As he and Hoo went off to find the tallest tree in all the Friendly Forest, Blaze started wondering if this was a wise decision.

When they got to the tree, Blaze looked up. He closed his eyes and asked the Maker to help him make a wise choice. Immediately, Blaze knew what to do—and not do.

"Hoo, I don't think trying to fly is a wise choice."

"I think you're right," hooted Hoo. "These are top-quality wings, but even so, you're still a bunny."

"Yeah." Blaze frowned.

"You might not be able to fly on your own, but do you-hoo-hoo want to go for a quick ride with me?" asked Hoo.

Blaze absolutely did. So, Hoo lifted Blaze up, up, up, and the little bunny got to fly that day after all.

Talk About It

- What was the unwise decision Blaze almost made?
- Have you ever made an unwise decision? What happened?
- Read James 1:5 again. What do we need to do to get wisdom?

Think About It

God wants us to make wise choices because He loves us. Do you have a decision to make right now? Ask God to give you wisdom, and He'll give it to you!

Pray About It

Dear God,

Please give me wisdom. Help me make wise choices that honor You, and help me live the best way, even when it's hard.

Amen.

DAY 27

Flora's Lost Scarf

Don't forget to do good and to share with those in need. These are the sacrifices that please God.

HEBREWS 13:16

Flora searched frantically for her green scarf. The scarf was nowhere to be found in her den. Her Cleanup Crew shift was in ten minutes, and it was getting cold. *I really need my scarf,* she thought as she headed out the door.

"Have any of you seen my green scarf? I *need* it," Flora asked her friends, who were hanging out in the tree fort. No one had seen the scarf, but they offered to help her go look.

"I see it!" Blaze announced. "Over there by the Babbling Brook!" Flora walked over to check it out. As she got closer, the scarf hopped.

"That's not my scarf. It's a frog!" exclaimed Flora. "Thanks for trying, Blaze."

"There! There!" hooted Hoo. "It's green and fuzzy and . . . Oh, never mind. It's just some springy turf moss."

A gust of cold wind blew through the trees. Flora shivered. "What if I never find it?"

"Look! Over at Frontier's Field!" Cubby shouted.

The friends hopped, scampered, and flew over to the pile of soft green fabric. Wrapped up tightly inside Flora's scarf were three field mice.

"Aw, what cuties!" said Flora. "They must have been so cold. I thought *I* needed my scarf, but it looks like these little mice need it more than I do. They can keep it."

Hensley scurried toward her friend. "That's super nice, Flora. And you know what? I just got some new yarn, so I can knit you another scarf!"

"Thanks, Hensley," replied Flora. "You sure are a great friend."

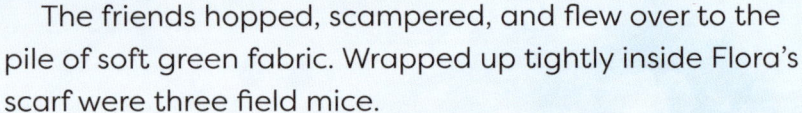

Talk About It

- What did Flora end up doing with her green scarf?
- How does it feel to share what you have with others in need?
- Why does God want us to share with others? Who could you share with this week?

Think About It

We can share all sorts of different things with others. We can share our time, resources (like money, clothes, toys, and so on), and talents. And best of all, we can share the good news about Jesus and His love for us!

Pray About It

Dear God,

Thank You for sharing so much with me. Please help me do good and share what I've been given with those in need.

Amen.

DAY 28

Hensley, You're Not Forgotten

If a man has a hundred sheep and one of them gets lost, what will he do? Won't he leave the ninety-nine others in the wilderness and go to search for the one that is lost until he finds it?

LUKE 15:4

It had been a long day of cleaning and rebuilding. The creatures of the Friendly Forest were doing double or even triple the number of volunteer shifts. And the forest friends needed a break.

After a few rounds of freeze tag in the Murky Marshland, Hensley decided to sit out. She was the slowest one, and she didn't like being "it" all the time. She watched her friends laughing and having fun without her. *It looks like they forgot all about me,* she thought.

A few minutes later, Cubby called out, "Break's over!" The friends all hurried back to continue their work, leaving Hensley behind. "Now they really forgot about me!" Hensley cried.

As the darkness set in, she began to cry even harder. "Why did we have to go all the way out into the Murky Marshland?"

Then she heard rustling in the bushes nearby. "Who's there?" Hensley asked shakily.

"Hensley!" Papa Hedgehog shouted.

"Papa! You're back! How did you know I was here?"

Her dad gave her a big squeeze, prickles and all. "I went to find you with the Cleanup Crew, but your friends thought you went home. I knew you weren't at home, so I came looking for you."

"Oh, Papa, I love you."

"I love you too, Hensley. And just so you know, thanks to the Maker, you're never, ever forgotten."

Talk About It

- Why was Hensley feeling forgotten early in the story?
- Even if we feel forgotten by others here on earth, who will never, ever forget us?
- How does it feel to know that God, your Maker, will never forget about you?

Think About It

You can read the full parable of the lost sheep in Luke 15:1–7. Remember that no matter what, God will never forget about you!

Pray About It

Dear God,

Thank You for never, ever forgetting about me. When I feel forgotten by others, please remind me of Your love. I love You.

Amen.

DAY 29

The Forest Friends Find Hope

May the God of hope fill you with all joy and peace as you trust in him, so that you may overflow with hope by the power of the Holy Spirit.

ROMANS 15:13, NIV

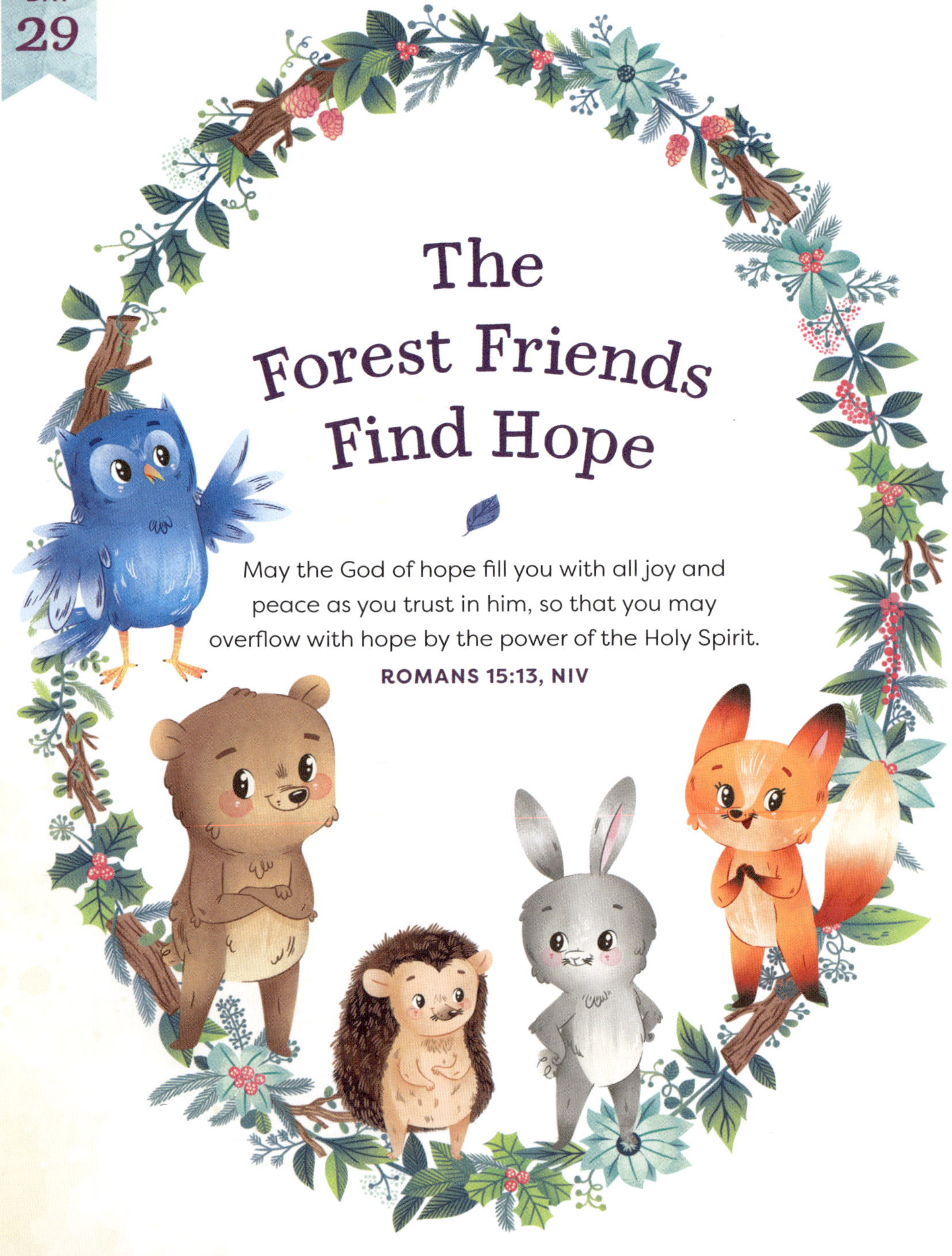

Wind rustled the few remaining leaves on the trees of the Friendly Forest. The hope everyone had felt seemed to have disappeared, and the wind felt cold and cruel. Homes were half-built, the food storehouses were empty, and the creatures were packing and saying their goodbyes.

"Be sure to pack enough food to tide us over on our journey," Grammy Bear said.

Cubby added another jar of honey to his pack. He couldn't believe they were actually leaving the Friendly Forest. He needed to find his friends to say goodbye.

Cubby found everyone sitting together in the tree fort.

"What if we never see each other again?" cried Blaze. Tears began to well up in all the friends' eyes.

"Even if we never come back to the Friendly Forest, there's still hope," said Cubby. "Grammy says the Maker always makes a way for hope—even when we can't see it."

"Maybe we could pray for more hope?" sniffled Flora.

The animals bowed their heads, and a feeling of peace and joy spread throughout the tree fort. As the friends exchanged hugs, they heard a loud commotion outside.

They hurried to the lookout and saw an entire army of creatures crossing Frontier's Field. They didn't seem to be coming for a battle, though—so why were they here?

Blaze raced toward the field to learn more. "It's the creatures from the Western Woodland!" he shouted back to his friends. "They are here to help! But they need places to stay."

"How about the tree fort?" said Cubby.

"Yes!" the friends all shouted with joy and so much hope.

Talk About It

- Why were the forest friends feeling hopeless?
- Do you ever have a hard time feeling hopeful about things?
- Even when things seem hopeless, who can help us always be hopeful?

Think About It

Remember, God can give us hope in all situations. He will fill you with joy and peace when you trust in Him!

Pray About It

Dear God,

Thank You for being a God of hope, peace, and joy. If I'm ever feeling hopeless, please remind me of who You are and fill me up with Your hope!

Amen.

DAY 30

The Friendly Forest Celebrates!

This is the day which the Lord has made;
Let's rejoice and be glad in it.

PSALM 118:24, NASB

It had been almost a month since the animals from the Western Woodland arrived in the Friendly Forest. The trails were now fully reinstated, the homes were rebuilt, and the winter garden was full of growing vegetables.

Cubby, Flora, Blaze, Hoo, and Hensley looked around at their beloved home as they headed toward sounds of music, fun, and laughter. The Friendly Forest sure wasn't the same as before the storm. It was even better!

Now winter was here, and along with it came an unusual but welcome buzz of excitement.

As they hopped, scampered, and flew to the celebration, they saw delicious food covering the tables—which of course included trays of goodies from Grammy's Bakery. Bright decorations and twinkling lights adorned the trees. Games were being played, and joy could be seen around every corner. A huge THANK YOU banner hung across the North Bridge to show everyone's gratitude toward the new friends from the Western Woodland.

"It's sure been a crazy year of change," said Cubby.

"Yeah, we're all taller!" Blaze stood on his tippy-toes and pointed his ears toward the sky.

"That's right, Blaze," agreed Hensley. "We certainly have grown. And we've changed in lots of other great ways too!"

"I've changed for the better thanks to all of you-hoo-hoo," Hoo added. "But I think the good we've seen in and around us mostly has to do with the Maker."

The friends all nodded in agreement.

"It has *everything* to do with the Maker," said Flora. "Absolutely everything."

Talk About It

- Why were the creatures of the Friendly Forest celebrating?
- What were some of the good ways the forest friends changed throughout the stories?
- What's one way you've changed as you've learned more about God and His love for you?

Think About It

Thank God for who He is and what He's done in your life. We all have something to celebrate. You just might need to throw a party too!

Pray About It

Dear God,

Thank You for creating me and loving me so much! Help me find ways to celebrate Your goodness and love. I love You!

Amen.

Amanda Jass loves helping families bring fun and faith into the everyday through her work as a children's writer and illustrator. After several years serving as a kids' ministry curriculum developer, she continues to grow in her passion for teaching kids all about God's love for them. Amanda's recent work includes her role as the general editor of the *Go Bible,* and she is the author of *Discovering Christmas,* a kids' Advent devotional. Amanda has a master's degree in education, and she lives in the Midwest with her husband, their three girls, and their little-but-loud dog.

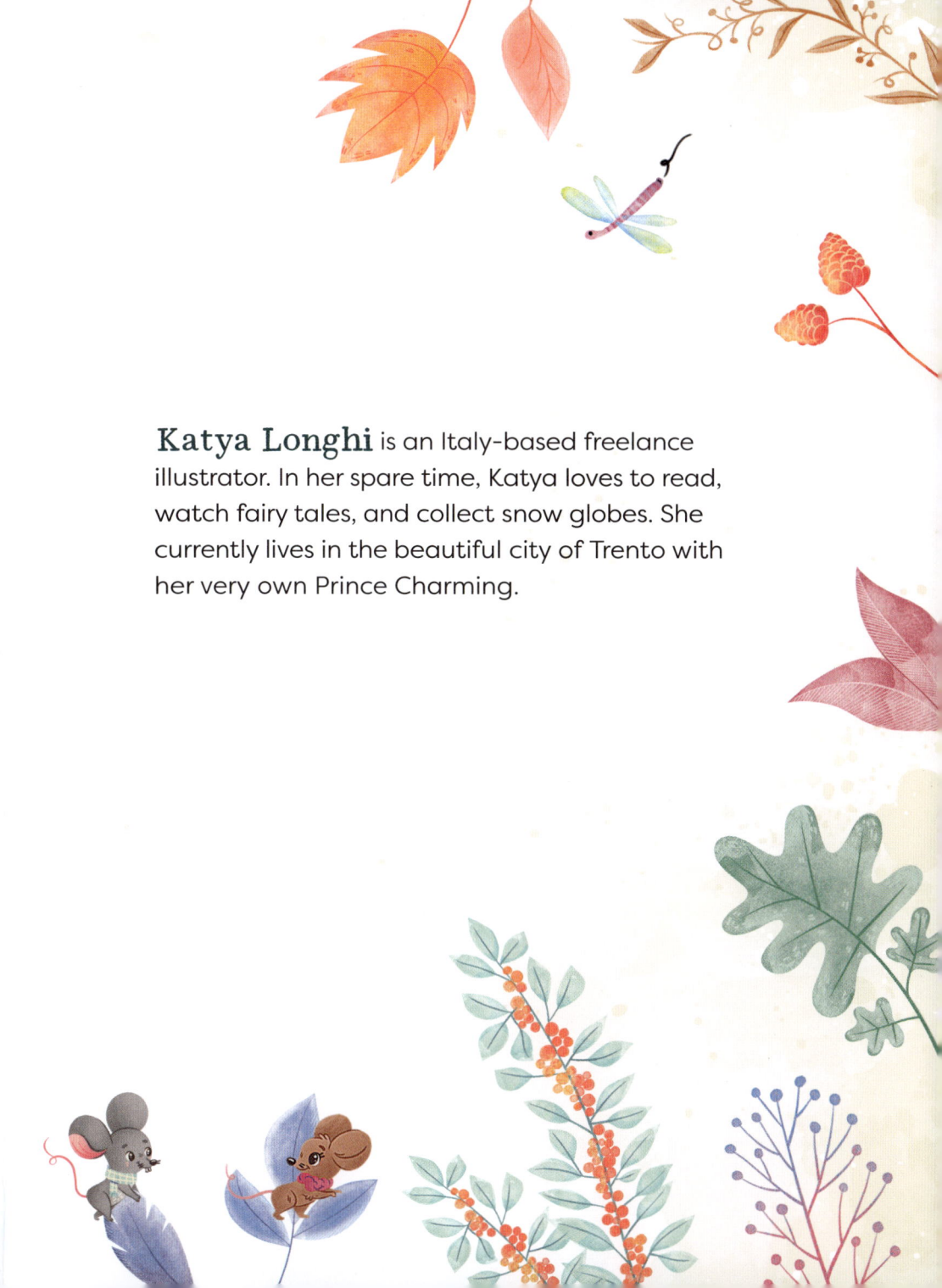

Katya Longhi is an Italy-based freelance illustrator. In her spare time, Katya loves to read, watch fairy tales, and collect snow globes. She currently lives in the beautiful city of Trento with her very own Prince Charming.

WATERBROOK

An imprint of the Penguin Random House Christian Publishing Group, a division of Penguin Random House LLC

1745 Broadway, New York, NY 10019

waterbrookmultnomah.com
penguinrandomhouse.com

All Scripture quotations, unless otherwise indicated, are taken from the Holy Bible, New Living Translation, copyright © 1996, 2004, 2015 by Tyndale House Foundation. Used by permission of Tyndale House Publishers, Carol Stream, Illinois 60188. All rights reserved. Scripture quotations marked (ICB) are taken from the International Children's Bible®. Copyright © 1986, 1988, 1999, 2015 by Thomas Nelson. Used by permission. All rights reserved. Scripture quotations marked (MSG) are taken from The Message, copyright © 1993, 2002, 2018 by Eugene H. Peterson. Used by permission of NavPress. All rights reserved. Represented by Tyndale House Publishers. Scripture quotations marked (NASB) are taken from the (NASB®) New American Standard Bible®, copyright © 1960, 1971, 1977, 1995, 2020 by the Lockman Foundation. Used by permission. All rights reserved. (www.lockman.org). Scripture quotations marked (NIRV) are taken from the Holy Bible, New International Reader's Version®, NIrV®. Copyright © 1995, 1996, 1998, 2014 by Biblica Inc.™ Used by permission of Zondervan. All rights reserved worldwide. (www.zondervan.com). The "NIrV" and "New International Reader's Version" are trademarks registered in the United States Patent and Trademark Office by Biblica Inc.™ Scripture quotations marked (NIV) are taken from the Holy Bible, New International Version®, NIV®. Copyright © 1973, 1978, 1984, 2011 by Biblica Inc.™ Used by permission of Zondervan. All rights reserved worldwide. (www.zondervan.com). The "NIV" and "New International Version" are trademarks registered in the United States Patent and Trademark Office by Biblica Inc.™

Text copyright © 2026 by Amanda Jass
Cover art and interior illustrations copyright © 2026 by Katya Longhi

Penguin Random House values and supports copyright. Copyright fuels creativity, encourages diverse voices, promotes free speech, and creates a vibrant culture. Thank you for buying an authorized edition of this book and for complying with copyright laws by not reproducing, scanning, or distributing any part of it in any form without permission. You are supporting writers and allowing Penguin Random House to continue to publish books for every reader. Please note that no part of this book may be used or reproduced in any manner for the purpose of training artificial intelligence technologies or systems.

WATERBROOK and colophon are registered trademarks of Penguin Random House LLC.

Hardcover ISBN 978-0-593-79805-8
Ebook ISBN 978-0-593-79806-5

The Cataloging-in-Publication Data is on file with the Library of Congress.

Printed in China

9 8 7 6 5 4 3 2 1

First Edition

The authorized representative in the EU for product safety and compliance is Penguin Random House Ireland, Morrison Chambers, 32 Nassau Street, Dublin D02 YH68, Ireland. https://eu-contact.penguin.ie

BOOK TEAM: Editor: Bunmi Ishola • Production editor: Laura Wright •
Managing editor: Julia Wallace • Production manager: Linnea Knollmueller •
Copy editor: Tracey Moore • Proofreaders: Carrie Krause, Rachael Clements •
Art director, book designer, and cover designer: Lisa Schneller Bieser

For details on special quantity discounts for bulk purchases, contact specialmarketscms@penguinrandomhouse.com.